THE RAIL

THE RAIL

BY

HOWARD OWEN

THE PERMANENT PRESS
SAG HARBOR, NY 11963

Library of Congress Cataloging-in-Publication Data

Owen, Howard
The Rail / Howard Owen
   p. cm.
ISBN 1-57962-043-4 (alk paper)
1.Hit-and-run drivers--Fiction. 2. Baseball players--Fiction.
3. Fathers and sons--Fiction. 4. Ex-convicts--Fiction. I. Title

PS365.W552 R35 2002
813'.54--dc21   2001036617
                                    CIP

Printed in the United States.

THE PERMANENT PRESS
4170 Noyac Road
Sag Harbor, NY 11963

Grateful acknowledgment to Max Gartenberg, to Judith
and Martin Shepard and Elise D'Haene.
Love and gratitude to Karen Van Neste Owen, a friend to
all writers and this one in particular.

Even before the stone and wood begin falling, people run outside, not dead, not annihilated, to find out who and what has been destroyed instead of them.

They dash into the giddiness of survivors, anticipating themselves on the evening news, or even CNN, eager to wonder aloud what happened and why, and what carelessness or wickedness made it occur, to see in what way they are superior to those dead and maimed, as yet unknown.

"I bet it's the high school," a man just removed from the hardware store says to a younger woman who was just parking her car. "Thank God it's not a school day."

"The Lord was looking after them," she says, shading her eyes. "Somebody must have been killed, though."

And they stand there, bonding in disaster, watching with everyone else as the thick smoke rises to merge with low-hanging clouds to the north. Then their strange rain begins, joining the drizzle that has chilled them all day.

At first, they notice the dust, along with what might be clumps of clay. Then come pieces of wood, none large enough to be of much danger, but adequate to send most of the curious under roof. Only the holiday-happy teen-agers, the boys primarily, stay outside to seek thrills.

It is the stone, though, that they all will remember.

No larger pieces reach the town itself, where a hail of pebbles peppers Dropshaft Road and the tops of houses for several seconds afterward, playing a discordant tune on tin roofs.

It is not the native red brick of which almost everything substantial in the area is built, but something grayer, older.

People will later claim there was a smell, musty and dry-rotted.

As soon as it's safe, many will venture closer, as close as they're allowed, and most will return with large and small stone fragments gathered from the roadside or in front yards. What they bring back exhibits precise angles hewn by men instead of nature.

That night, with no coordination, without even speaking of it, members of almost every family in the older part of town will have a piece of somber ancient stone sitting somewhere in the living room or den, something to which a person can point for validation while telling the story.

ONE

IN THE SKIPPED beat of a heart, the deer is gone, a dun-colored memory swallowed whole by the November woods.

Other than the windshield, there is only the swiftly fading sound of the animal's frantic burst through the hollies, tulip poplars and white oaks to vouch for it. Even with the leaves off the trees, the deer already has blended into the camouflage forest by the time the two men jerk their heads to the right. The glass is shattered, a spider web in the late-afternoon sun. The car, Neil sees, had stopped as if of its own volition, with no remembered slamming of brakes, half on Castle Road, half on the shoulder that dips gradually into a shallow ditch.

David is sitting with both hands on the wheel, staring straight ahead.

Neil is borne back to their first driving lesson, something that hasn't crossed his mind in many years. It happened just before he ceded that tender responsibility to David's mother, to everyone's relief. They had only gotten as far as the first intersection of their suburban street, where David (after weeks of practicing in their driveway — endlessly back and forth, as limited in his movements as an engineer on a one-track train) had panicked and been unable to find the brake until they were 20 feet beyond the stop sign, the ensuing jolt throwing them into the steering wheel and dashboard.

Neil either spoke forcefully (his words) or yelled (David's tearful accusation later). They somehow got the car out of harm's way, and Neil is fairly certain he himself drove them home, defeated as they sometimes were.

Today, he puts his hand on his son's right knee and tells him it's OK, no harm done.

David jerks his knee away.

"OK, my ass! Look at that shit! God damn . . . What . . ."

He's sputtering, still trying to make sense out of it.

Neil takes his hand back. He figures the deer must have struck the slant of the windshield with one bounding hoof; he sees now that there is a dent on the hood, probably from the only other impact the animal made. His analysis: They're lucky as hell. The deer could have rolled through the windshield, into their laps with its slashing hooves. But then, he thinks, it isn't my car.

"I heard somewhere," he finally ventures after a long silence, still no other cars in sight along the winding road, "that those things kill more people than bears or snakes."

David looks at him as if he has just offered pertinent information about the moons of Neptune. He shakes his head and reaches for the key in the ignition. The car starts on the second try, and the rear wheels are able to pull out of the soft, sloping dirt and onto pavement.

Before shifting into forward and driving on, David strikes his fist against the steering column.

"Nine months. Nine damn months I've had this car. I can't believe this shit."

"Do you have insurance?" Neil realizes it is a stupid question as soon as he asks it.

"Of course I've got insurance! Jesus, do you think I'm an idiot? But it's just one more thing, one more hassle I don't need right now."

Neil is silent then. He doesn't know why he said as much as he did. If he's learned nothing else the past two years, he's learned the safety and strength of silence.

In the three hours from Mundy to Penns Castle, they've spoken very little. In the scramble to see who, if anyone, was willing to retrieve Neil Beauchamp, David emerged as a last-minute dark horse, one on whom Neil himself would have placed very long odds. His money had been on either Blanchard, who is not supposed to drive, or a Greyhound bus.

Neil appreciates the gesture, appreciates almost anything at this point. He's never been much of a talker, though, and while he supposes David must have developed above-average language skills along the way, he has not often practiced them on his father.

"I love you, Dad," he said to him once, nearly a decade ago, "but I don't like you very much."

The occasion was David's wedding reception, and Neil suspected the rare moment of clear-channel communication was inspired by too much champagne and David's then-new wife.

Neil had thanked him for clarifying their relationship, a little uncomfortable with both halves of it. He would have been easier then with the concept of liking without loving.

Now, this late in the game, he would settle for either. As a fallback position, he would be willing to take a quiet porch and a little stand of woods where he could walk around, kicking up leaves like a kid, watching squirrels chase each other around big oak trees, sitting on a stump with no one else in sight. This, he hopes, is what Blanchard and the late James Blackford Penn IV are offering.

David never visited him and wrote only twice. When Neil was told that his son would take him away, he figured it was just one more last-minute piece of chain-jerking, or some bureaucratic miscommunication, until the new burgundy-colored car pulled up at the gate and his son got out.

On the way to Penns Castle, Neil asked about Carly and "the girls," unable on short notice to remember their names.

"Frannie and Abbie are both fine," David responded, coming down just hard enough on the two names to let Neil know the gaffe was noticed. "Frannie's loving first grade, and Abbie is already starting to read."

Neil assumed that Frannie must be about six and that Abbie, the younger one, would be four or five.

"I didn't learn how to read until I was seven," he said, and then there was a good half-hour with nothing but the radio.

"Why," Neil asked finally to break the silence, "are you doing this?"

David shrugged. "Well, I had some owed days coming. Figured I might as well spend some quality time with my old dad."

His smile was a little crooked as he said it, twisting to the right, and Neil realized that this was David's smile almost forever. It was the smile that said, "This is OK, but nothing lasts. We're doing all right now, but I know things will turn to shit in the end. You can't fool me. I'm wise to it all." Neil would like to go back to the day his son's straight-up, open grin started listing to one side.

By the time they turned off Route 56, they had established little more than the fact that David would be staying at Blanchard's for a few days as well, leaving on Wednesday to be home for Thanksgiving, that everyone was healthy, that Virginia Tech was going to a bowl game and the University of Virginia wasn't, that yahoos and rednecks were running the state.

Neil observed that a large piece of the Virginia woods on the southeast corner of the Castle Road intersection had been rather violently cleared. The deep red earth was stripped except for a solitary sycamore tree, its presence only serving to remind Neil of what had been there. The hill, which once offered only tantalizing glances of the flatland below, to the Richmond city limits more than five miles away, now left nothing to the imagination. Neil could see what appeared to be a large mall in the far distance.

On the bare acreage, bulldozers and large trucks surrounded the footings of something large and rectangular.

David took notice and shook his head, but Neil supposed he had no real basis for comparison. They never visited Penns Castle much back then. How long had it been since his son had been here?

"Nineteen-seventy-three," David said, and Neil wondered if he had been talking to himself.

And then the deer had interrupted them.

Back on the road, they are almost at the castle's entrance when an old red pickup truck approaches from the opposite direction. Its driver slows and then stops dead in the road, blowing the horn and waving his arm.

"It's Tom," Neil says, then adds, not sure David remembers, "your uncle."

"Half-uncle," David corrects him, and it's clear to Neil that David wants only to continue the few dozen feet to Blanchard's and end this joyless trip, but he does as his father asks. There is nowhere to pull off, but Castle Road seems not to be the route of choice for the citizens of Penns Castle any more. Tom's truck is the only other vehicle they've seen since they left the state highway.

"I thought you two would be getting here about now," Tom says as he hops out of the truck. "I was going down to Blanchard's to see if you'd made it."

He stares at David's damaged car.

"Good Godalmighty. You all must have hit a deer. I bet it was Dasher. We can get that fixed tomorrow."

"No," David says, getting out of the car, "I don't believe it was a reindeer."

Tom looks confused, then says, "Nah. That's what Ray's little girl, Rae Dawn, calls him. She seen him munching on her grandmomma's shrubbery one morning before the rest of 'em had got up and said to Millie, who was making breakfast, 'Look, Gramma, it's Dasher.' She's all hepped up over Christmas."

And then, almost as an afterthought, Tom gives Neil a hug and shakes hands with David, whom he hasn't seen in almost a quarter of a century.

"You've grown up a lot," he says to his nephew, looking him over. "I remember when we used to take you down to the lake. Remember how much you hated them worms?"

Tom laughs at the memory, his ruddy face turning redder under the John Deere cap. It is, Neil sees, a memory David has not grown old enough to laugh over.

The fall David was 10 or 11, after the season was over, the three of them came down from Cleveland. It was a warm October, and Tom, just 12 years older than David, wanted to take his nephew over to Lake Pride, fishing.

David had never been fishing. It was a spring and summer thing, and by the time Neil was out of baseball, the opportunity for all that was long gone. Neil himself had never been fishing or hunting much; his main memories from his youth in Penns Castle were playing sports and working in William Beauchamp's store. Tom, though, was a fool for fishing.

Neil went with them down to the lake; Tom brought three cane poles he had made himself. He'd already dug up some fishing worms.

They parked along the dirt extension of Castle Road and walked in a couple of hundred yards to the lake, through a million of the thorn thickets that seemed to seize every undomesticated thing in Penns Castle. By the time they saw water, Neil and his son were both bleeding from a hundred nicks.

Neil knew immediately that it wasn't going to work. David probably saw the reddish-brown worms, two or three inches long, as miniature snakes, surely nothing a sane person would ever pick up. He looked at his father as if for help, Neil remembers, and he offered none, only encouraging the boy to pick one up, assuring him that they "won't bite you."

Neil wanted the boy to do something difficult. He feared already that David would never be Dave, the fearless, freckle-faced son of the Virginia Rail, destined to break every record the old man ever thought about. David's timidity irritated him.

"Go on," he urged, picking up one of the wriggling worms himself. He impaled it on the hook, challenging the boy, who already knew what was expected of Neil Beauchamp's son. David did actually reach into the old Maxwell House coffee can and gingerly lift out one of the smaller specimens. After dropping it twice, he almost succeeded in spearing it. What he managed to do, finally, was stick the hook in his finger.

"Hey, David," Tom had said, "I'll show you they won't hurt you. Watch this." And he picked up the biggest one he could ferret out of the can, put it up to his mouth, bit it in half, and then swallowed both halves.

Neil looked at his half-brother in amazement, then burst out laughing. David, his finger bleeding impressively, turned and ran.

They called after him, laughing still, and it was a few seconds before they realized that he wasn't coming back, that he was running in a direction that would not take him back to the car, or the road, or anything else except more thorns and mud and Virginia forest for the next five miles.

It took them two hours to find him and coax him back. He was almost hysterical, his clothes torn, his face and hands a patchwork of scratches. By then the idea of taking David fishing — then or ever — had long since been abandoned.

Now, Neil can see in his son's eyes that David hasn't forgotten a bit of it.

"Yeah, Tom," he says, forcing a smile, "I'm still not much of a fisherman. I went to college so I'd never have to bite a worm in half."

Tom laughs, refusing to take offense. He barely graduated from high school, but Neil knows he's turned William Beauchamp's old mom-and-pop operation into a thriving hardware store, making a good living off the new homeowners in their 3,000-square-feet houses down by the lake where Tom used to fish.

Tom Beauchamp, Neil has long believed, is a perfect fit for the family and the place where he was born, blessed and not even knowing he's blessed, just happy to be here. He was too small to do what Neil did, too uncoordinated, and he didn't make good grades in school like the girls, but he has probably never for an instant doubted his course.

Tom is 50 years old. To Neil, he has never seemed as old as his chronological age, has never even seemed grown, to tell the truth. Never married, he's spent much of the last 10 years in the company of a woman two towns away who seems no more interested in a wedding than he does.

"Ain't that a shame about the trees?" he asks them both, pointing in the general direction of the bare earth. He tells them about the new DrugWorld that's supposed to go there, "a superstore."

"It's going to put Tim Rasher right out of business," Tom says. Neil knows the Rashers have run the pharmacy in Penns Castle longer than he has been alive. "It's going to make Castle Road a mess, too. Blanchard's fit to be tied."

At the mention of her name, Neil tells Tom they'd better be going.

"I think Millie's got something planned for tomorrow night," Tom says before they go. "She'll call you."

When Neil and David get back in the car, Neil looks over at his son.

"Last chance," he says, quietly. "You can drop me off at the front door and be back in Alexandria by nightfall, free of all this mess."

David doesn't look at him.

"Is that what you want?" he asks his father.

There's only the slightest hesitation.

"No. No, that's not what I want."

"Then neither do I."

And that's how they leave it. David drives the short distance to the stone sign that says "Penn's Castle." The sight of the transplanted English manor house is a shock even to Neil, who grew up in its shadow.

"Well," David says when they stop in the circular driveway, flashing his crooked smile, "we're home."

TWO

THE SUN WAS still shining low and fierce through the trees on Castle Road. But on the slight downhill slope to the house itself, Neil and David sink into the twilight that steals a half-hour of daylight from the ridge's eastern slope.

They sit for a moment after David stops in the circular driveway.

"I'd forgotten about this place," he says. "It sneaked up on me. I remember, now, how damn big it seemed when I was a kid."

Neil has to twist his head to see the peak of the roof from the Camry's low window.

"It's still pretty big."

In the fast-closing darkness, as he eases out of his son's car, Neil doesn't see her at first.

She must have been standing in the stone archway, half-hidden from them.

"Neil."

He's holding his gym bag, the same one they took from him two years ago and returned this morning, its contents untouched, when she steps forward and hugs him, a crystal glass of bourbon in her hand. She spills some on his back and then tries to wipe it off.

Neil can't think of anything to say, just holds the embrace for several seconds, until she asks him isn't he going to introduce her.

"Ah, David, I'm not sure you remember this lady, but she's your aunt, or half-aunt. . . ."

"Or half-assed half-aunt," Blanchard says. "You've grown up handsome, honey." She steps forward and shakes hands, then gives him a hug as well before stepping back and regarding his damaged car. "Deer?"

David nods. He remembers meeting her only once before, not long after the fishing-worm fiasco. She was then, he somehow recalls, Blanchard Penn Worthy, and she spent a night with them in Chagrin Falls, probably the last year his father played for the Indians. He remembers how beautiful she was, how bright and wild her eyes were, how she had such perfect blonde hair. She was wearing shorts and a halter top, and he would have erections for weeks thinking of her, of how she flirted with him. But he remembers, too, hearing her cry that night, many drinks later, when it was just the adults out in the living room, before he knew much about divorces. His mother was a strong woman, and it unnerved him to hear their guest in such ragged, hoarse, blatant agony.

Later, his mother told him that Blanchard had a lot of problems.

Today, he figures she must be in her mid-to-late 50s, but in this light, at least, she is still a fine-looking woman, firm and blonde enough to be 20 years younger.

"Let's go inside," she says, then turns to lead them past the arches and up the steps into Penn's Castle, the crystal glass hanging sideways and empty in her right hand. "I need a drink."

David fetches his one small suitcase and follows them.

Blanchard guides them along the cold stone floors, then turns right and finally stops in front of what will be David's bedroom. Across the wide, tall hallway is another room, Neil's. The ceilings here are at least 20 feet high, but there are floor vents, indicating that someone has, somehow, gotten central heat installed to fight the cold and damp that the walls themselves seem to be breathing on them.

She makes sure they can find the great hall and from there

the sitting room, then says, "You all look like you need something to cut the chill," and goes toward the kitchen.

"Just Coke for me," Neil calls after her.

Half an hour later, they're all seated before a roaring fire in a room surrounded by two floors of Penn's Castle, the one above them bordered by a walkway. The ancient stone, carried across an ocean for Blanchard Penn's great-grandfather, is set off by wood paneling from another world. There are bookcases everywhere. The room appears to be the size of a small house, and the five chairs drawn around the fire, surrounding one small coffee table, are overwhelmed.

Still, the fire is warm. David has two bourbons; his father insists on soft drinks, and David thinks Blanchard, who has matched his two plus whatever she drank before they arrived, pushes him too enthusiastically to have another.

The lights in the room — and, David has noticed, in the hallways, bedrooms and bathrooms — are no match for the November night. There is barely enough illumination for reading. But his chair is comfortable and the day has been very long, and soon he is as comfortable as he's been in weeks. He is near nodding off when Blanchard, who has been filling Neil in on her move back to the town and the castle, turns to him.

"So, David," Blanchard says, "you must have a very exciting life. Covering Washington politics and all."

David gives her a vague but affirmative answer, staying away from specifics. He is not yet ready to tell his father, let alone his half-aunt, that he actually is only a Washington newspaper correspondent in the loosest sense of the word, one who is at present, as one acquaintance unkindly but accurately put it, being paid not to write.

This leads Blanchard to tales of a long-ago liaison with a United States representative "from one of those little states; I think it was Delaware," and from there to tales of her former life in New York.

Neil's back is used to hard, unyielding furniture, and he squirms to find a comfortable position in the armchair that holds him. He looks around the large room, and his eye is drawn to a row of items on the mantel high above the fire that Blanchard occasionally feeds. He sees (and in squinting to see realizes that, for the first time in his life, he probably doesn't have perfect vision) that they are minie balls, standing, with their conical heads and the horizontal lines on their sides, like forgotten soldiers on the dark wood.

They might be the same ones, Neil thinks, that he used to play with, so long ago. How else would they have gotten here?

He was, in the days when he was still Jimmy Penn, allowed the run of this place, as the accepted son of the resented daughter-in-law (who would become the even more resented ex-daughter-in-law).

Before he was banished, Jimmy was indulged in various ways. His favorite pleasure, though, was The Box.

In the last days of the Civil War, the town, which was still called Dropshaft, had been the venue for a small action on the path of Lee's final retreat to Appomattox.

On the hill where Penn's Castle would be built, the battle's hard debris can still be found — belt buckles, buttons and minie balls, used and unused. When Neil was Jimmy Penn, the Penns already had, for generations, been throwing these remains of the Battle of Dropshaft into a large wooden box, once used for stovewood. They were fond of collecting things.

By the time Jimmy came along, The Box was a young child's treasure trove. He would, playing by himself (for no other children in his town were allowed in Penn's Castle), ferret out the least damaged of the bullets and align them in rows and columns, facing each other like the two armies to which they had belonged. He would be the great Stonewall, or sometimes Moseby or even Lee, and the hated Union troops would always be vanquished. He only knew their names and pictures and that they were gods who were somehow thwarted.

He was four years old the last time he was invited to Penn's Castle.

Virginia, the socialite, had joined his father; they stood before him in the big room — this room — where he played with his tiny soldiers. The James Blackford Penns were still living there, with James' mother. They looked down at him from a great height (the Virginia Rail, that six-foot-three shard who tore up the American League, got his height from the Penns) and said nothing for a while.

The boy, still Jimmy Penn for a few more weeks, was used to a range of emotions at Penn's Castle that went from tolerance to adoration. That day, though, he sensed something was different. Looking up, he saw them both frowning, and the look his father's wife had was approximately the one he'd seen when the mouser had shown up with four unexpected and much-uncelebrated kittens.

"Jimmy," his father told him, "let's go for a walk."

It had been a day like this, blustery and bright. Jimmy Penn wanted to stay inside and play.

"Come on, son," the man said, and his voice seemed to catch on the last word. Jimmy put on the overcoat his grandmother had bought for him and followed his father reluctantly outside.

They sat on the steps, and James Penn told his son that they couldn't see each other "for a while," that Jimmy was getting a new father now and would have to stay with him.

Neil figured, years later, that his father's new wife wanted no part of him from the start but needed the thin moral authority of his mother's remarriage to get James Penn to slam the door on him entirely.

"Why can't I stay with you?" the boy asked that day, and James Penn looked across to the woods and told him. "Because your mother wants you to stay with her all the time. You're her little boy now."

The boy whined and tried to cling to his father, and James Penn finally grabbed him by his shoulders and held him at arm's length, bending so they were eye to eye.

"You're hers now," he said. "You're hers and William Beauchamp's. You're not mine any more."

Jimmy Penn threw the biggest tantrum he'd ever thrown or ever would when his father wouldn't let him back in the house with him. Jimmy was left to scream and kick the kitchen door from outside until, a few minutes later, James returned with a handful of the minie balls.

"Here," he said. "Take these back and play with them. It's just for a little while, Jimmy. I promise." Even then, an old servant had to help James Penn get him in the car and back to his grandfather O'Neil's house.

It wasn't a little while, either. One day, when Jimmy, who was now Neil Beauchamp, was six, his stepfather threw the minie balls away, tossed them down one of the old abandoned mineshafts in the woods behind the store, and told Neil he was too old to be playing with toys. Neil was much older before he broke himself of the habit of going back into the woods behind Penn's Castle and spying on the human transactions at the house where he once was adored.

"Neil?"

He's aware that Blanchard has been talking to him.

She has a look on her face as if she's about to cry. "You seem so far away."

"No," he says. "I'm right here."

"I was just saying that Millie and Wat wanted to come by and see you tonight, if that's OK. I told them to come about eight."

It isn't all right, but Neil doesn't feel like arguing, is out of the habit of resisting plans and orders, has gotten used to going with the flow. He shrugs his shoulders.

"You've lost some more weight," she says. "It looks good on you." She gets up quickly, and Neil supposes he should follow her into the kitchen, where she's taken their three empty glasses. But he doesn't.

David, who has sunk so low in his chair that the top of his head does not clear its back any longer, looks over at his father.

"Is she OK?"

Neil Beauchamp shakes his head, says nothing.

"This is amazing," David says, looking up as if he's just now discovered the incongruity of Penn's Castle. "I remembered it as being big, but I never really went near it until today."

The Penns had moved to Richmond by the time David was born. The castle was abandoned, half-obscured by young pines and hollies and thorns, surrounded by a barbed-wire fence and vandalized within an inch of its life before he ever visited the town or saw the house.

"She just moved back here last year," Neil tells his son. "She's still got some work to do."

"You can say that again," they hear Blanchard call from the kitchen, and Neil remembers how the old place was always supposed to have "zones," as the Penns called them, where you could hear a person a room away, whispering.

"It's getting there, though," she says, coming back in with two bourbon-and-waters and a Coke balanced on the tray. "It'll soon be as good as it ever was. Wait and see. We're going to be so happy here."

David looks at his father. Neil shakes his head so slightly that it escapes Blanchard's eye. He sees that the drink she brought in for herself is half-gone already. While he's trying to find a polite way to tell his benefactor that she's had enough to drink, she gets up and walks quickly to the back of the room, where glass doors face out into the U-shaped rear of the house, two long wings flanking what seems to be, as the outdoor light comes on, a garden.

"Cully!" she calls. "You come here, Cully! Time for supper." She whistles and slaps her knee, looking worriedly into the dark.

"What kind of dog do you have?" David asks her, as Neil looks away.

"Cully's a beagle," she says, not looking back at them. "He's a mess, too. One of those high-strung 13-inch ones. Sometimes I have to call him for half an hour before he'll come to me. Cully! You get in here right now!"

Neil rises, unsteady despite being the only one in the room who's sober. He walks over to the door and takes Blanchard's hand, pulls her gently back into the room and closes the door.

"Let me take care of Cully," he tells her. "I'll fetch him after a while."

Blanchard listens, bites her lip for a moment and then nods.

"Well," she says when she gets back by the fireplace, picking up another piece of split oak and throwing it into the flames, "I suppose you all are starved."

She leads them into the dining room, toward a table for perhaps 14, its burled elm legs nicked where they stick out from under the tablecloth. Neil and David help her, carving the beef roast and setting the table.

"Do you want me to go see about the dog?" David whispers while Blanchard worries over peas and beans and checks the bread.

His father looks at him and shakes his head.

THREE

NEIL AND BLANCHARD are out of practice at making dinner conversation; David is tired from the long drive and welcomes the silence. The dead hush, broken by nothing more jangling than fork against china or the mantel clock's quarter-hour chimes, is so deep that he feels he might fall into it and wake up sometime tomorrow.

He misses Carly, whom he has already called, and the girls, and he suspects he would soon grow to miss the din of the television, the CD player, the always-ringing telephone, the competing, escalating needs of a six-year-old and four-year-old. Tonight, though, he is glad for the quiet.

David glances over at his father, who looks neither right nor left, certainly not up, as he devours everything in front of him, as neatly and efficiently as a military-school cadet. If someone had told him, three months ago, that he would be escorting Neil Beauchamp back to the free world, that he would care enough to do such a thing, he would not have believed it.

He is not a forgiving person by nature. He has, he supposes, inherited his mother's sense that right should be rewarded and, implicitly, that wrong should be punished, and furthermore that failure and all it begets fall within the spacious boundaries of wrong.

When David was young, it was his father, the great Virginia Rail, whom he always felt he was letting down. The fly balls he missed, the all-star teams he didn't make, the athletic determination he didn't exhibit, all of these disappointed his father, David knew. Looking back, though (and the last 10 weeks have given him more time than he ever wanted for reflecting), he is willing to believe that Neil Beauchamp got over his disappointment soon enough, that he always (if sadly) accepted the fact that his only son was not going to be a great baseball player.

Neil would treat him roughly, yelling at him on occasion, hurting his feelings on a regular basis. But Neil Beauchamp's great crime, David believes now, was neglect. He would forget birthdays and anniversaries, fail to show up for father-son banquets and school spelling bees, flatly refuse to do overnighters with the Boy Scouts.

Catherine Taylor Beauchamp filled the spaces, and it seems now to David that she did it willingly. She was, everyone agreed, a trouper. David seldom wanted for a parent when one was required, but there were many events where Kate was the only mother in a room full of fathers.

She would defend Neil in his absence, and everyone in Chagrin Falls understood that the Virginia Rail sometimes had things to do that mere mortals were spared. Should someone make a remark that could be interpreted as pejorative concerning the Rail (as David himself has come, over the years, to refer to his father, with no hint of reverence), Kate would respond with a smile that reminded more than one errant suburbanite of a large predator, and then make the speaker understand certain things that should have been understood already. ("Well, you know, Neil had to be at that Cystic Fibrosis fund-raiser last night in Akron, and he's got to fly to Chicago tomorrow to pick up some kind of award or other, I can't remember what just now. He's a little tired." And the nearly visible subtext: "And who, exactly, are you, Mr. Nobody, to be making cracks about the inestimable and much-in-demand Virginia Rail?")

Later, though, age and arthritic knees started catching up with Neil Beauchamp. David was in his teens, and suddenly his mother was uttering the same kind of asides that would have brought down her wrath on some hapless outsider two years before. And David was as uncomfortable in this role of reluctant confidant as he'd ever been in the previous one — the kid who would never be the man the Virginia Rail was.

After David left for college, he came home as seldom as he could.

It had been Kate Beauchamp's wish that her son, after it was determined that he would never wear a major-league uniform, would go to law school and make use of the fine intellect he'd been granted in lieu of speed and reflexes. And when David let himself fall by the wayside in the competition as an undergraduate at Columbus, when he "drifted," as Kate described it, into journalism and newspapering, "getting by" with barely passing grades and spending too much of his time working for the campus paper, a certain chill let him know that he, too, had fallen short.

He still sees his mother twice a year, once with Carly and the girls, once without. It is clear to him that, at some deep-seated level, he has slipped from the pedestal, has committed the crime of non-brilliance.

At least, he's always told himself, his mother was there. When, after the glory days, Neil would be the manager of some minor-league no-hoper (which inevitably did worse with the Virginia Rail than it had the year before without him) or the third-base coach at Texas or Seattle, Kate was there, through his high school and college years, hectoring him at close range or long-distance, always there.

What, he wonders to himself in his 38th year, is worse: to be neglected or to be disappointing? He has been sure, for most of his adult life, that he would rather be disappointing. Lately, though, things have been happening.

He knew about the consultants, of course. They were, according to his friends back in the newsroom in Cleveland, crawling all over the place "like cockroaches," trying to justify the million dollars the company was paying them for a year's fine-tooth combing to find out how the paper might turn its 20 percent yearly profit into 25 percent.

"How hard is that?" asked a woman who had been a city-hall reporter since David was in high school. "You fire people and get your news off the wires. Screw quality; no profit center there. But you've got to have somebody to tell you to do it, so it isn't your fault. Pontius Pilate would have used consultants. 'I'm sorry, Mr. Christ. It isn't our idea, but we paid these consultants a lot of money, and they said we could maximize profits if we nailed your ass to this cross.'"

As the Washington correspondent, David felt blissfully above all that. He commiserated with his colleagues when he was back in town, and by phone and e-mail at his office in D.C. But he'd never even seen any of the consultants. When they announced the first round of layoffs and buyouts, which were referred to first as downsizing and then rightsizing and finally as career growth opportunities, he went to a tearful party for two friends who were among those cut.

Even when the assistant managing editor started mentioning the "next round" being a little closer to home, David never worried that much. He'd been with the paper 10 years and had won several state awards, had even been nominated for a couple of Pulitzers. Granted, he'd not won anything in the last three years, maybe was in a little bit of a rut, but he'd stand on his record, as he told Carly, who took it all more seriously than he did.

When he was called back to Cleveland in September, he told his wife not to worry, but even he was worried by this point. The first wave had cut almost 10 percent of staff, and now they wanted more.

The meeting was held in the human resources office. The sign was newer than the ones on the other doors in what the newsroom referred to as the beancounter wing. The department's old name, Personnel, had been considered too cold and unfeeling.

The director of human resources was a man two years younger than David. His name was Tad Winkler, and he was as universally despised as anyone in the entire company. He never smiled, but he never frowned. He wore neutral-colored suits (no one had ever seen him in anything except a suit) and small, brown-framed glasses. He was of average height, average build, as mild as a lamb. His job was, it seemed to David, to do whatever needed doing that no one else was willing to do.

"Winkler," someone had said at the going-away party following the first round of cuts, "was born in the wrong place, at the wrong time. I'm thinking Germany, nineteen-thirty-nine. He's great at following orders."

By the time the meeting was over, David was no longer an employee of the newspaper. He would be given six months' severance, the director told him. David kept thinking that at any moment, the assistant managing editor, or the managing editor himself, would come bursting in and tell Tad Winkler there was no way he was going to be allowed to fire David Beauchamp, who had done such a wonderful job for so many years. Soon, though, he came to understand that he was alone, and he was screwed.

He'd always thought, when he allowed himself the dark fantasy of being in this position, that he'd spring across the desk and throttle the living shit out of the godless humanoid on the other side, something he and old cronies would laugh about 20 years later in some bar in some other city. When it was over, though, he realized, when he shut the door quietly behind him, that he had issued only a minor complaint, so seamless was the process, so devoid of any criticism of anything David might have done or not done. ("The consultants say, David, that we've reached a point where this paper can no longer afford to have a Washington bureau, for now, although certainly that could change. We know we need a Washington correspondent, but they are adamant, and the corporate people agree. We are working on the most generous packages we can offer, especially for valued employees such as yourself. You will be well-provided for.")

David never saw the assistant managing editor again. He went back to the hotel, answered no calls, flew home, and made one more trip back to Cleveland, to clear up the particulars of his benefits package.

In the final analysis, he didn't even blame Tad Winkler, who was doing what he had always done and always would do. He forfeited the thin hope of future employment at the paper when he sent his two immediate bosses 30 dimes each for Christmas.

Carly took it badly, then seemed to recover. Their townhouse in the Old Town section of Alexandria had a mortgage far too heavy for them to carry past the middle of March, when the checks from Cleveland would stop coming, but she soldiered on.

The depth of his problem would manifest itself to him slowly. Carly was always telling him how much she loved him, and he was always quick to respond. He had lived in a family where the word "love" didn't get used often enough, and he thought it couldn't hurt to say it as often as possible.

In the weeks of September and then October, though, he detected a change in the old familiar pattern. Where she had been the one to say the first "I love you" before (to which he always responded, almost always enthusiastically), now he found that often she was headed out the door, going to show houses or to shop, and his unprompted "I love you," which he had to admit sometimes sounded almost desperate, tagged after her like an abandoned puppy. And her responding call seemed to be diminishing into nothingness. Sometimes she said (in what seemed to him an almost-impatient tone, as if she resented the delay to her departure) "Love you." Sometimes, the echo from Carly was so short and devoid of vowels that David thought it might have fit well on a vanity license plate: LV U.

And there was the oral sex.

Carly had been an enthusiastic sexual practitioner since their dating days, and she was, in general, an athletic, good-natured partner, willing to try new things and perfect the old ones. One of David's favorite sexual memories, one that could arouse him whenever he thought of it, was of a vacation trip they'd once taken to San Francisco. He had suggested, after they drank the complimentary sauvignon blanc in their hotel room, that they try something "a little different."

What he wanted her to do, he said, was let him pick her up. He told her to go down to the bar and wait there for him. He would pretend to be a salesman, in town for a convention, and she would be at the same convention, but they would never have met before.

"I'll start coming on to you," he told her, nibbling her ear and then sliding his tongue inside it. "I'll say all kinds of outrageous things to you, and you'll pretend you want me to stop, but you won't really. We'll go farther and farther. And then I, a complete stranger, will take you back to my room and fuck you silly."

She seemed to lean into his tongue a little.

"Am I married?"

He hadn't thought about it.

"Yes," he said, reaching around her from behind and sliding his fingers over her nipples. "You've got a trusting husband back in Virginia who you'd never think of doing all these nasty things with."

They determined that David was married, too, and before Carly headed out the door, she sat down on the bed and wriggled out of her pantyhose and panties, leaving them on the floor.

"Who knows?" she said, and the look she gave him made him want to throw her on the floor right there, half in the room and half out. "I might get picked up by some stud salesman."

After they had played their game, getting each other hot enough in the hotel bar to draw stares, he took her back to the room, unbuttoning her blouse on the elevator and taking it and her bra off while they were still in the hall outside. They made love all afternoon.

They played the game twice again, both times when they were out of town. It was part of what made their marriage work, David thought, that they played so well together.

Sometime in October, though, David had wanted to have mutual oral sex, and Carly had said she didn't feel like it. He asked her again a few days later (and he never remembered having to ask before, not really; it pleased her as much as him, he had always thought). She said no, and now he was too proud to ask again. And the fact that something was not the same as it was, that there were limits, made it all different. They'd had straight, missionary-style sex just three times in the past month.

Now, in the tenth week of his unemployment, after getting maybe-laters and nothing-nows from half the newspapers with Washington bureaus, he is starting to suspect that he has drifted into the land of Wrong and must be punished.

David wonders how much of it is Carly and how much is him accepting his status. He remembers how it was when he was a kid, and he'd have a B on his report card when it should have been an A, or he'd want to go outside and play before he had done his homework or some chore. The disapproval hung like smoke from a burned dinner, and he would do anything, anything to redeem himself.

He was always letting The Rail down, too, he could see, but his father would get over it, not through any strength of character, but because there was always something else coming along to distract Neil Beauchamp. David has always half-blamed his father, half-blamed himself for the fact that they were not usually interested in the same things. If he had been a better ballplayer, or if he had at least worked harder at being above-average, he's fairly certain The Rail would have paid him more attention. But he has always blamed his father for not caring more, and he wonders if Kate Beauchamp was so judgmental toward him to compensate, or if Kate and Neil were just a case of opposites attracting.

David has tried to learn from what he experienced. When he was actually being paid to produce articles for the Cleveland paper, he would miss interviews, sometimes to the detriment of his job, to "be there" for Frannie and Abbie. He always insisted on giving them their baths and reading them bedtime stories, showering them with attention even before he became a temporary house-husband.

Last week, though, something happened that made him think about his life plan, his whole philosophy of using The Rail's paternal skills as a reverse compass.

Frannie learned to read before she was five. Now, in the first grade, she is something of a prodigy, even by over-achieving professional Washington standards, adept at the computer, comfortable with numbers, learning cursive script.

David and Carly figured the bed-wetting would have stopped already. Even Abbie had stopped. But almost every other night, there was the same scene, now David's chore to clean up.

When he came in to wake her up Wednesday morning, after she had two dry nights in a row, and the bed was soaked again, he scolded her, told her that she'd have to do better, then just caught her eye and glared until she looked away. All through breakfast, he didn't speak, and then all the way to the bus stop, where she stood a few steps away from him, not playing with the other children as she usually did.

That afternoon, he sat her down when she got home, and explained to her that this was not something big girls did, that if she wanted Daddy to be proud of her, she must stop wetting the bed. She bit her lip and nodded, then went to read a book.

Dinner was quiet that night, and when David finally tried to cheer Frannie up, she just seemed nervous. She went to her room early.

He awoke sometime after two to go to the bathroom. On the way down the hall, he heard something, and when he went into the girls' room, he could see, from the hall light behind him, Frannie turn quickly away and feign sleep.

He walked over and sat quietly on the side of her twin bed. He put his hand on her shoulder.

"What's wrong?" he whispered. His oldest daughter kept her eyes tightly closed, then finally spoke, with her eyes still shut.

"Nothing."

"You ought to be asleep. Don't you feel well?"

She turned over, eyes open now, her look nailing him like a deer in the headlights.

"I don't want to go to sleep. I'm not ever going to sleep again."

David started to tell her how silly that was, when he realized why she had said it, and what willpower it must take for a six-year-old to stay awake that long. And he wanted to cry. Before he could beg forgiveness, before he could tell her that he'd be glad to lie down beside her, and if she wet the bed, he didn't care, she had turned over to face the wall.

He left the room and didn't sleep much that night.

What he thought about, then and the next brooding day, was how much that scene resembled one he and his mother had played out more than 30 years before.

He also thought about the last letter he'd gotten from Neil Beauchamp, who was getting his parole. David made a couple of phone calls.

That night, he told Carly (and it was the first time lately he'd had the will to actually take a stand on anything) that Frannie would quit wetting the bed when she quit wetting the bed, to not worry about it and let him deal with the sheets, since he had nothing else to do.

But first, he told her, he had to leave for a few days.

He had to go and retrieve the Virginia Rail, who might or might not be worth the effort.

FOUR

Neil and David are helping Blanchard wash the dishes when the doorbell rings.

"That would be Wat and Millie," she says, drying her hands with a paper towel.

She opens the front door, the men two steps behind. From the greetings, and the observations about paint jobs, the new fence and lost weight, Neil sees that they haven't been in each other's company for some time.

"And Neil," Millie says, saving him for last. She lets it stand at that, squeezing his arm a little. "It's been a long time." Wat mumbles something and shakes hands somberly, as if greeting the next of kin at a funeral.

More than two years, for sure, Neil resists saying. Hell, that's how he'd told them he wanted it. The week before they sent him to Mundy, he'd called everyone he knew who might have had the urge to visit and ordered them not to. Everyone except Blanchard took him at his word.

They sit around the great room, Blanchard trying to keep the conversation alive. Neil is struck, not for the first time, by the difference in his half-families.

When he was a schoolboy, the geometry teacher would make them draw circles with their compasses, perfectly round, sometimes intersecting each other at two points or, if the distance was exactly right, just one, the curved lines from the Number Two pencil lightly kissing each other at their one common ground. That is how Neil has long thought of the Penns and Beauchamps. He is that point, touched by two otherwise-independent entities.

The Penns are (were, except for Blanchard) tall and thin, adept at parlor conversation but too reserved, really, for the backslapping, half-jolly, half-mean spirit Neil remembers pervading his childhood in the Beauchamp household.

"The Penns," William Beauchamp said once (and no one thought he meant it in a sympathetic or admiring sense), "are just too good for this world." The Beauchamps were (and are) keen-eyed merchants, never giving anything away, never owning up to good fortune for fear it might abandon them, always talking poor in the style of the put-upon subsistence farmers they once were.

Blanchard is, despite all the bourbon and wine, cool and undistracted (her distractions not coming principally from any bottle, Neil knows), dressed smartly in clothes from Ann Taylor, the reds and tans just right for her, the hair perfect without hinting at great effort to make it that way.

Millie, seven years younger than Neil, has gained weight since he last saw her. She was never as pretty as Willa, who came two years later, and now she seems to have passed the point where she really cares about being fashionable. She seems to be settling.

She and Wat appear to be comfortable. Neil doubts either of them has had any more regret than brother Tom over staying in Penns Castle. They dated in high school, got married in the Oak Grove Baptist Church within sight of the brick rancher William Beauchamp bought after the war, and then built their own house, a place from which to watch their children and now grandchildren thrive.

They believe, although Neil knows they would never say it to her face, that Blanchard and all Penns are frivolous, high-handed people, undeserving and pretentious. Neil finds it strange that Penns Castle is the domain of the Beauchamps now, with three generations building a stronghold while

Blanchard stands alone in Penn's Castle itself. She (whose family gave the town its basis for existence and then its name) is the come-here; they are the original settlers who know the language she has forgotten or never knew.

They talk about nothing much at all.

"Tom said he saw you this afternoon," Wat offers after a silence that seemed to David at least five minutes long. "Said your car got messed up pretty good by that deer."

David nods his head.

"Did you hear what Rae Dawn calls him?" Millie says.

"Who?" Blanchard asks.

"Dasher," David replies, his eyes closed.

"She is the cutest thing. I can't wait for you to see her. Which reminds me: You are both — all three — invited over to our place for Thanksgiving dinner."

Blanchard and David both say they can't make it. Blanchard has not, from what she has told Neil, been inside any of the Beauchamps' homes since she moved back, and he imagines she is not at all sure the invitation now is sincere. David tells them he plans to leave on Wednesday.

"Better let me have somebody look at that car tomorrow, then," Wat says.

"Oh, come on, Blanchard," Millie says. "Everybody's going to be there. Willa and Jack, and their kids, and Tom. What's one more plate, honey? We're all family here."

Neil would do almost anything to avoid being in what he remembers as a small dining room full of loud adults, with their equally loud children at the card tables set up in the living room, a television football game blaring, the many dishes passed around so slowly that it is impossible to have an entire, intact, hot meal. He has missed good and plentiful food, but he craves a quiet place more.

He sees that there is no getting around this, though, and if he is going, he wants Blanchard to be there, too, a wish he conveys to her across the coffee table. She accepts.

"Well, good," Millie says. "Come on over about three."

"Can I bring anything?" Blanchard asks.

"Oh, no, honey. That's OK. I'm afraid that whatever you fixed would be too fancy for that crowd. We're just going to have some plain old turkey and dressing and such."

Blanchard is quiet. Soon, not more than 45 minutes after they came in, Millie and Wat rise to leave.

"Well," Blanchard says while she's still waving to them and smiling as they circle around and head back toward the road, "I guess I'll just have to forgo the *pommes allumettes, magret de canard* and *mille-feuilles.* We're going to eat some good, honest Amurrican food."

David smiles as they turn to go back inside.

"How," she asks, when she turns to Neil, "did you keep from killing them when you were growing up? I'll bet neither one of them even visited you once. They act as if they don't owe you a thing. . ."

She stops in mid-sentence, then continues, blushing and clearing her throat, "Well, I don't suppose I'm quite the one to be talking about debts, am I?"

The town was first called Dropshaft because of the mines.

Coal was discovered there in Colonial times, a horizontal seam that ran west and south from the James River, so that, 100 feet and more beneath the surface, there was enough of it to warrant nearly-vertical holes. Fearful immigrants already were descending into those holes by the late 18th century.

By the time the first James Blackford Penn had assumed control, due to the untimely death of his father in a rather democratic cave-in that claimed him and 15 Italian laborers while he was inspecting one of the shafts, the mines had been generous for some decades and seemed to be quite literally bottomless pits.

He felt secure enough by 1856 to do something even the swells down in Richmond could appreciate: He bought a castle and had it sent to him. Technically, it was a manor house, but for all who saw it afterward, it would be Penn's Castle.

The house was in danger of being torn down where it stood in the English Midlands, where one less unheatable 16th century dwelling was not considered tragic. James Blackford Penn, whose ancestors had come to America penniless from the approximate area in which his future home was located, heard about it through a friend, the man who built the railroad connecting the mines with the river below the falls. The man traveled to England once a year, and when he told James Penn this story, Penn wrote, wired, then sailed over himself. Thus he started the wheels in motion that would soon result in an entire Tudor estate, every stick of wood and every stone, being packed, hauled to Southampton and shipped to Norfolk. From there, it was taken up the James, finally loaded onto wagons and hauled up the hill to Dropshaft, where it was reassembled.

They planned to continue calling it Pittscomb Hall, but almost everyone knew it from the first day, from the time the stones started rising atop the red Virginia hill, overlooking the mines that bought it, as Penn's Castle. James Penn, perhaps desiring some immortality from his purchase, soon joined the majority.

He had the old brick house beside it torn down, and he and his wife gave the Fourth of July party that officially inaugurated Penn's Castle in 1858. A drunken guest wandered off the grounds that day, and his body was not found until, a week later, buzzards circling one of the abandoned mines alerted one of James Penn's slaves.

By the time the fourth James Blackford Penn was born in 1913, Reconstruction and diminishing coal had reduced the

Penns' station somewhat, but they were still by far the richest people in their town, whose name they had succeeded in changing to Penn's Castle, after its only distinguishing aboveground characteristic, in the 1870s. Various highway departments and general ignorance of punctuation caused the town's apostrophe to disappear sometime before the First World War.

Two generations earlier, a James Blackford Penn probably would never have been allowed to marry an O'Neil. Even in the 1930s, it was barely within the older Penns' endurance level.

It was, though, the Depression, and the mines were closed for good. The Penns still could live, for some years, on their fortune, but the more far-sighted could envision a future in which this would not be so. Such a realization made the Penns perhaps more egalitarian, made it more palatable for James Blackford Penn IV to fall in love with and marry an O'Neil, Jenny, the daughter of the mines' last manager, who was now trying to make a living at farming in the flat land below, along Pride Creek.

When Jenny O'Neil was in high school, she took a job working at the little restaurant in the rail station on Dropshaft Road. The 20-mile line, once used for hauling coal, had been bought by the Penns and was the only working remnant of their empire. It transported people down to Richmond and back, connecting there with the main north-south line, and provided some dependable income. The restaurant was in town, where the tracks of the Penn and Richmond ended, and everyone came there to gossip and see who got off the train.

James Penn worked there in the summers, between semesters at the University of Virginia, and that was where he fell heedlessly in love with Jenny O'Neil. His family and hers thought they would get over it, because he was only 19 and she just 15 when they started seeing each other. They were attractive together, with his dark, lean, quiet, patrician Penn-ness complementing her soft, mischievous presence. She was blonde and a foot shorter than he, with a wide, sensuous mouth, a ready smile and a body that was fully and lushly adult.

He seemed more smitten with her than she with him, but when he proposed the day after he was graduated, a week after she had finished high school, she agreed. They eloped to North Carolina. When they returned, after the Penns had recovered, they moved into Penn's Castle, where there was room for 10 such couples.

Almost from the start, Jenny felt greatly outnumbered in the company of James, his parents, his two sisters and a pair of maiden aunts, living in what her father referred to as "King Coal's Second-Hand Castle." The birth of James Blackford Penn V on March 5, 1935, seemed to help, seemed for a while to shore up his parents' rickety marriage.

In the end, though, it wasn't enough.

James had been a young 20 when he proposed. He discovered, after his son's birth, that there were other young women, some with more growth potential than Jenny O'Neil. Jenny's only growth that he could see was of the more obvious, physical sort. He noticed, for the first time, that her parents were both what he thought of as squat people, and he wondered how a graduate of a fine university could have failed to foresee the effects of a relatively easy life and good, ample food on a young woman unused to either and barely five feet tall.

She ate, James Penn's mother noted to one of the aunts, "as if meat and potatoes would be prohibited forever within the hour." She gained 10 pounds before getting pregnant, added another 20 before Jimmy's birth,and lost almost none of it.

James Penn began catching the eyes of other young women, who seemed likely to gain in beauty and worldliness. He saw in those eyes sympathy for one so obviously above (literally and figuratively) the round woman sometimes at his side.

He began to make business trips to Richmond, where he often spent time with women whose families' stock was similar to that of the Penns — old money going slowly down, relatively new money still rising. His mother knew some of this and was not entirely offended by it.

Jenny knew, too, and for a time she was determined to endure it, because her day-to-day life now included so much that she never had before and would never have again. Her hands, like the rest of her, became soft. There were still servants.

What finally sent Jenny O'Neil Penn away, and eventually into the arms of William Beauchamp, was cards.

When she first moved into Penn's Castle, she noticed that there were unopened packs of playing cards everywhere she went. She saw them as a sign of careless wealth. The Penns liked to play bridge, and they had apparently decided that never again would they be without a fresh deck of cards. They were everywhere — inside drawers in rooms all over the house, somehow in nooks of the attic, atop the mantel and on the bedside tables. She once found a new pack under the seat on the passenger's side of James' Ford.

Jenny, who had learned something of penny-ante poker from her father, determined that she must learn bridge.

But while the Penns, with their large hands and quick minds, seemed made for the game, Jenny struggled. She was prone to drop cards and to shuffle them badly, and she tended to get absent-minded, especially after a couple of glasses of Mrs. Penn's sherry.

Her game seemed to diminish after the birth of her son, and there were nights that ended quite literally in tears of frustration.

The last hand of bridge Jenny O'Neil played with the Penns was in late January of 1937. There had been a foot-deep snow that started the afternoon before and was only now abating. Everyone had been indoors all day, and the closeness was wearing on them. Jimmy had been sent to bed early after his whining had caused one of the aunts to wonder out loud if "that child" was ever going to learn any manners.

Jenny and the aunt were partners, against James and his mother. They had been drinking since dinner, and it was now past 10. In some way that Jenny herself never quite understood, she got spades and clubs mixed up in her mind, and when the inevitable annihilation from bidding on that assumption fell upon her and her partner, the aunt slammed her cards down.

"I believe," she said, "that it is more likely that your hands will grow large enough to hold the cards, my dear, than that your mind will grow large enough to play them correctly."

Jenny knew, when she let herself think on it, what the Penns thought of her in general and her bridge-playing in particular, but she had never before been so bluntly and openly insulted. And when she turned to James for aid, she caught him and his mother looking at each other and shaking their heads, smiling slightly.

She left the table, went to the bedroom where their son was not yet asleep, bundled him up and walked out the front door. James called after her, and she knew part of her was waiting for him to follow and bring her back. The long coat and boots she put on in haste and anger were no match for a foot of snow.

But he didn't follow her. He let her walk out the door with their son. Jenny could not remember it perfectly later, but she was almost certain she saw a quick movement by his mother, a hand on the arm to hold him back, as she passed them.

The moon, almost full, was shining hard and pale over the white blanket covering everything around Penn's Castle.

It took Jenny almost an hour to walk into the town itself, holding her son, then carrying him on her shoulders, once falling in a hidden ditch and sending them both tumbling in the wet, deep snow.

By the time she reached the railroad station where she had first met James Blackford Penn, it was after 11. The door was locked, but she still had a key from her days working there. It was another mile to her father's farm, so she let herself in, and that's where she and Jimmy spent their first night out from under the roof of the Penns.

The next day, she got a ride to the O'Neil house on the morning run, because the engineer knew her. She had cut herself falling, the blood only flowing after she got relatively warm inside the station, and now she had a bandage around her right leg. Her eyes were so swollen from crying and lack of sleep that her father first thought she had been beaten and was ready to fetch his rifle and walk up the hill to do what he had wanted to do for some time.

But Jenny O'Neil's bruises were mostly on the inside, and her father's sensibilities were not fine enough to appreciate and sympathize so much with those. James Penn never really tried to get her back, and they were divorced within the year. Before another year had passed, James was married to Virginia West, of the Richmond Wests.

After a short period of open hostility, Jimmy was allowed to visit with his father's family from time to time. It was hard for Jenny to keep her son, who was now talking, from unfavorably contrasting his new life on the farm with his former one. Mealtimes in particular were apt to be unpleasant. Each complaint by the child was taken as a declaration that the Penns would never have served such fare.

The Penns might have kept Jimmy. After all, he had their name; he was the roman-numeraled link to all that had made them what they were.

But two things worked hard against little Jimmy Penn.

* Jenny, a year after James Penn and Virginia West were wed, accepted a marriage proposal from William Beauchamp, who ran the store in Penns Castle, and who hated the Penns even more than Jenny did.

* His father's new wife wanted nothing in the world less than the small reminder that she was not the very first Mrs. James Blackford Penn. She wanted, as she told her husband, "our own family."

What Neil Beauchamp has never known (and it is a mystery that has been so washed over by so much time that it is but a small grain, no longer even a pebble, that only occasionally rubs, like the tickle in the throat from a departing cold) is whether his mother acted more from love or spite in keeping him, and whether his father was ruled by a desire to please his new wife or by a wish to have the past, and most especially Jimmy Penn, disappear.

FIVE

TUESDAY MORNING, David awakens to solid, metallic thuds that shake his bedstead. The steady beats, a second apart, last for several minutes, stop, then start again. David lies under the covers in the chilly room during the silences, waiting for the pounding to resume.

Finally, he gives up, rises and hops across the cold floor to retrieve his clothes. When he comes down the hall toward the kitchen and dining room, he hears Neil and Blanchard talking, and as he makes the final turn and comes into view, 20 feet away, he sees his father looking downward. Blanchard's right hand is resting on his left.

Blanchard jumps slightly, and David has the feeling he used to get when he would come upon his parents in similar conferences before breakfast. He hated it when he walked in and found them talking like that, quietly but intensely, never offering to share any of it with him. They were always a little sad or angry afterward.

Blanchard looks as if she has been crying, but she gets up quickly, and the moment passes. She walks away, talking a mile a minute about pancakes and sausages and "a real Southern breakfast," as if his and Carly's Alexandria townhouse were part of some other country. Neil turns to look out the window into the backyard.

David remembers something from the blur of the previous evening.

"Did the dog ever come back . . . Cully?"

The kitchen, through the open door, goes quiet for a second. Neil looks up and shakes his head, the way David remembers now he did the night before, and he changes the subject.

Over breakfast, which does indeed surpass anything David has had recently — stacks of pancakes with real maple syrup, sausage, hash browns with onions, cheese grits, scrambled eggs, apples fried in butter, homemade biscuits — Blanchard clears her throat and speaks.

"I heard you ask about that dog," she says, with a short, loud laugh. "We've been playing that game for years, haven't we, Neil? We had that dog when I was a little girl, and once in a while, one of us will get up and call for that old dog, just like it was still here."

Neil nods, and there is no more talk of Cully.

Blanchard says that she can take care of the dishes while they go in search of a shop that can repair David's car.

"I expect Garner's can fix it. I know they replace windshields," she tells David, then gives him directions: down to Route 56, then half a mile toward Richmond, on the right.

"You remember Garner's, don't you, Neil?" she asks.

He shakes his head.

"We've got to get you reacquainted with your old hometown. You wouldn't believe all that's springing up."

She frowns, biting her lower lip. "Of course, all of it isn't good. Like that goddamn DrugWorld."

She goes on to tell them, her voice rising, about the "bane of my existence," the source of the piledriver that woke them both and the stripped earth they noticed the day before.

"They sneaked in there and got it rezoned commercial 10 years ago," she said, banging a coffee cup on the oak table. "That was right after Henry Waller bought the land for just about nothing from the Simmses — you remember the black family that lived out there by the highway? And it was before anybody from Richmond had even thought about moving out here.

"Of course, I'm sure Henry Waller knew they were going to develop Lake Pride, because he and Jimmy Sutpen are thick as thieves, and Jimmy's a county commissioner, and half the damn lake is on his property anyhow.

"They all look out for each other, and they all get rich, and they don't care what happens to the land and the trees."

David doesn't suppose the time is right to mention how the Penns made their money, not with his mouth full of Blanchard's breakfast.

Neil puts one of his big, rough hands over both of hers.

Blanchard, her guests learn, has been leading the hopeless fight to keep the large drugstore chain from clearing the woods ("they've already done that") and building a store that, she says, will surely run the one in town out of business. She and a few dozen townspeople ("mostly newcomers, plus poor Tim Rasher, of course") arranged a meeting with the county commissioners, but they were told there was nothing that could be done, that the county needed more business.

"For what?" she says, her voice rising again. "We have all the drugstore we need. What we don't have enough of is woods. They're clearing this place faster than the Amazon rain forest. Nobody wants to raise taxes, so they just bring in more damn stores nobody needs."

She concedes that her opposition to DrugWorld probably is helping it win the town's approval.

"They think I'm a come-here," she says, looking amazed. "A come-here! There were Penns here when these monkeys were still in trees. No offense to Millie and Wat and theirs, Neil. But I could wipe the whole town out by advising them not to eat rat poison. Whatever I suggest, they do the opposite."

"I haven't quit yet, though," she tells them, smiling off into the distance as she carries dirty dishes into the kitchen. "I'm not out of tricks yet."

The car, David learns, was damaged worse than he had thought. Something has apparently come loose related to the battery, is Neil's guess, because this morning it won't start. David curses and kicks a tire. He has never been mechanically inclined and fears that things broken never will be fixed again.

They go back inside and call Garner's, which sends a tow truck. The driver tries in vain to jump-start the Camry, then hooks it (a little carelessly, David thinks) to the truck and pulls it the mile to the garage.

Blanchard offers to lend them transportation, so they can go to the shop "and maybe just knock around town. Maybe you could get some things at the grocery store for me."

Her only vehicle, it turns out, is a truck, "a big, red, shiny one."

"Well, I thought I ought to do something to blend with the environment," she says as she gives them the keys. They retrieve the truck from the old garage beside the house that is done in stone to vaguely resemble Penn's Castle itself.

"Want me to drive?" David asks Neil. "Or maybe you want to give it a shot."

Neil tells him no, not yet.

"Let me get my feet on the ground first."

So David carefully drives them out to the road. Every glint of sunlight, every limb moving in the breeze, he realizes, makes him flinch a little.

"Not much chance of hitting two in two days," Neil says.

"It'd be worth it to hit the same one again."

"You mean ol' Dasher?"

"Yeah. They'd probably throw me in jail. It'd be like killing Santa Claus."

They find, when they reach Garner's, that there's one tired, discouraged-looking mechanic at work, although another one is expected "any time now." David tries to stress the urgency of the task, but Neil remembers enough of how Penns Castle works to know the futility of trying to hurry anyone.

After he became a famous outsider, he used to chafe, on rare visits home, over how nothing could be pinned down. No task could be defined by hours and minutes.

"Let's go for a ride," he tells David, who shrugs and follows him back to the truck.

Before they can leave, a county sheriff's car pulls up behind them, blocking their exit, and a young man in a strikingly unstylish brown uniform gets out. He walks slowly over to the passenger's side and looks over his sunglasses. He resembles someone, Neil thinks, perhaps an old classmate's son.

"You Neil Beauchamp?" the deputy asks.

Neil nods.

"I thought so. Miz Penn said you all had come down here."

David and Neil say nothing, and neither does the deputy for an uncomfortable stretch.

"I just wanted you to know," he says at last, his voice slipping a little. "I just wanted you to know that Lacy Haithcock was a friend of mine. He didn't deserve what happened. Didn't deserve it any way, shape or form."

Neil nods again. He waits; he can see the mechanic, sipping a soft drink, standing to one side, watching. David starts to say something, but before he can, the deputy turns and walks quickly back to the patrol car, slams the door and roars away, the tires throwing dirt and rocks in his wake.

They sit in the truck, not moving, giving the man in the brown suit ample time to be somewhere else. Neil sighs and sinks into the seat.

"Better put on that seatbelt," David tells him. "I have a feeling that guy would like to take you in for something, anything."

This Neil does wordlessly, mechanically.

"Are you OK?" David asks him.

Neil nods.

"I guess you expected some of this."

"I deserve some of it."

David turns toward his father.

"Are you sure this is what you want? To stay down here, I mean. I know Blanchard says she's going to look after you, but . . ."

"Here's as good as anywhere."

"There are places where they don't know you, though."

Neil is quiet. Finally, as much to keep David from saying or asking anything else, he says, "This'll be OK. Best place I've had lately."

They head east, Neil directing his son. They cross Pride Creek where it runs north toward the river, a hundred-yard swamp that flows beneath the four-lane highway.

"Turn here," Neil directs at the next road to the right.

Dropshaft Road goes south, curving back toward the town of Penns Castle. It has been repaved since Neil last saw it almost three years ago, before he went away and before Blanchard moved back from the city. The thin, gray, hump-backed pavement has been covered by new blacktop, widened two feet on each side and flattened a bit. The lines are bright yellow and white.

Neil recognizes the farm where his mother brought him 60 years ago, after James Penn and before William Beauchamp. He has vague memories of disapproving adults and a dearth of toys.

"Your great-grandparents owned that farm," he offers. David slows down and pulls off on the now-ample shoulder. The house is still there, a quarter-mile back along a dirt road so rutted that the bottoms are lost in the shade.

"Can we go there?"

"I don't know," Neil says. He fears the chain across the rut road, fears anything that does not adhere to strict observance of the law.

"Come on," David says. "Nobody's going to care."

Neil shrugs. He gets out slowly and follows his son, looking left and right as he passes to the other side of the road, the first highway he has walked across in two years. He looks again to see if they're being watched as they disappear into the weeds, following the trail to the house.

The O'Neils, whom Neil visited often after his mother married William Beauchamp, lived in a two-story, wooden farmhouse with a tin roof, surrounded by 40 acres of stingy Virginia clay. When the last of Jenny O'Neil's sisters left home after half a life of serving her parents, married at last to a retired railroad man who had courted her for eight years, her mother moved with her. Jenny's father had died of a heart attack five years earlier.

In the past 20 years, since the mother died, the land has been sold, and Neil supposes that it, too, will someday be a parking lot with stores and cars, something else for Blanchard to fight. For now, though, it is abandoned, a dead farm waiting to be buried under asphalt. Empty bottles, graffiti and broken windows testify to squatters and hell-raisers and young lovers.

They look around inside. Neil, who never would come to such a place on his own, has not visited it in those 20 years. He doesn't expect to find anything that encourages memory, but he is surprised. Walking into the kitchen, where they all ate, he in a raised chair that had been his mother's when she was his age, he is amazed to see that there is a little plaque still hanging on the wall. It must have been left there that last day, when perhaps the aunt and her new husband and some friends were loading everything up in some Joad-like exodus.

The plaque and the wall itself have sunk into a gray-brown that seems to have sucked all the color out of the world. When Neil walks over to the rectangular tile, though, he knows what it is. When he rubs it with his fingers, the red and green shine through as if they had been protected all those years by the dust.

Neil says the words: "Them that works hard eats hearty." The plaque, brought back by someone on some long-forgotten trip, features a grinning, almost leering Amish farmer, fat and happy among fields such as the poor O'Neils never were privileged to own.

David stands next to him and says nothing.

Neil goes outside, holding the piece of tile, and sits on the rotting front porch.

David comes out and sits beside him.

"You know," Neil says, looking straight ahead, "you didn't have to do this. You sure as hell don't owe me anything."

"It's not like I'm here for keeps," his son replies, picking at a thorn that has gotten caught in his trousers. "I'm going back tomorrow.

"And," he continues, taking a deep breath, "it's not like I couldn't get away from my job."

Sitting on his never-met great-grandfather's front porch steps, David tells his father all about downsizing.

When he is done, he realizes he feels at least momentarily worse for letting this secret, this weakness, out in the world. Like passing gas loudly in public, the relief is more than wiped away by the shame.

But he also sees that it is not as hard to tell Neil as it was to tell his mother. He used the phone for that revelation, and there was only silence for too long on the other end. What David was forced to admit to himself, after their rather tense conversation concluded, was that Kate shared his conviction that he must have done something terrible to lose his job in such a way, that he had drifted, without knowing it until it was too late, into the Land of Wrong.

She probably believed — he hoped she believed — that this was only temporary, and not a sign that he was bound to follow his father, a man rarely spoken of by Kate (and then only as "your father") into the chartless swamp of squandered promise, doomed to disappoint the ones he loved.

Neil knows — he knew it then, really — that he was rarely there when David needed him. He conceded that, has conceded it to himself many times over the years. He doesn't wonder that David went years without seeing him. What amazes him is that his son is here now. The way Neil sees it, if you miss the first step and the diaper-changing and the first day of school and Little League and spelling bees and graduations, just because you're so important that you can be somewhere else and get away with it, and then you fall from grace, you deserve what your life has become.

"It'll get better," is all Neil can think to say. "You're a good writer."

David asks him how the hell he knows that.

Neil, the only inmate at the Mundy Correctional Center who subscribed to a daily newspaper in Cleveland, Ohio, just says he knows.

As they leave the O'Neil farm, they cross Pride Creek and then start the steep climb into town. The railroad tracks are to their left, used now only for Christmas-time excursion trains that fill with children outside the old Penns Castle depot (now turned into a restaurant named Penn Station). The trains travel five miles, then stop at a crossing closer to town, amid much squealing and cheers, so Santa Claus can board.

As David veers right near the top of the same ridge on which Blanchard's house sits a half-mile north, Neil sees that the holiday decorations are already hung over the town's main street. Thin rows of plastic greenery, festooned with red and silver bells, hang over them as they pass the first few hilltop houses and the old Presbyterian church. A couple of strands even hang over Back Street, which branches off to their right.

The newly-designated, freshly-painted Penn Station is to their left, surrounding the commercial center of the town. A sign hangs on its side, drooping a bit, advertising "All U Can Eat Lunch Buffet, $5.95."

Neil points out Tom's hardware store on the right, with the old Beauchamp place, the big frame house that is also Tom's now, next to it, followed by the post office and Rasher's Pharmacy. They pull into one of the diagonal parking spaces in front of the store. Three boys, perhaps 12 years old, walk past on the sidewalk, carrying skateboards. A gray-haired woman speaks to them, calling them each by name, and they answer her bashfully.

David gets out and looks down the street. Several buildings and houses away is the stop sign where Dropshaft runs into Castle Road. He can see the edges of the town in all directions, two more rows of houses along Back Street behind the hardware store, nothing much beyond the tracks on the other side. Something in the tidiness of the town — the ability to stand at one spot and see the post office, the fire department, the houses of friends and family, the greater part of your world — appeals to him, he tells Neil.

His father offers a short laugh.

"It has its drawbacks. At least, it used to."

Neil has never been a great storyteller. Kate complained often about his unwillingness or inability to "open up," and his childhood has never been his favorite topic.

Still, his son is here, and he doesn't have much to offer him except stories.

SIX

WHEN WILLIAM BEAUCHAMP appeared unannounced one evening at the O'Neils' front door, everyone except Jenny's father was surprised.

Gerald O'Neil and William Beauchamp had known each other for many years. The O'Neils were dependent on William and his father for credit when times were lean, as they often were.

When William had approached Gerald about the second daughter, the one who had the good sense to leave that scoundrel in his high-and-mighty castle, Gerald did not discourage him. William Beauchamp was 35 then, 14 years older than Jenny, and he was a little too heavy, and a little too pinched of countenance, in the way of someone who spends much of his life trying to keep woebegone farmers from turning his store into a charity ward, to be considered good-looking. He had not been married before. But William ran and soon would inherit an endeavor which, while never a threat to make the Beauchamps rich, had never failed completely the way Gerald O'Neil's farm always threatened to.

Gerald did not mention to his daughter that William Beauchamp was coming courting, but he did think this could not help but lead to better things for Jenny. With a sickly-seeming, whiny three-year-old and no prospects, she had scarcely been noticed by the younger men of Penns Castle since her separation and divorce.

The people with whom Jenny had gone to school were not naturally unkind, but her fall from the grace and ease of the castle did afford them some amusement. Someone made up a verse, and it soon made the rounds in the town and among the farmers along Pride Creek:

> *"Jenny O'Neill*
> *Went up the hill.*
> *She was too good to work.*
> *I bet now she will."*

Jenny allowed herself to be courted by William. She knew, even as they drew close to a wedding, that anything else would be unseemly, but that while she herself would be better provided for in her new life, Jimmy's future was somewhat unsettled.

The Penns still lavished attention on the child, and it was part of the O'Neil canon, repeated often as if to make it more real, that his rich father would provide for him "whatever is needed" in the way of clothing and education. He was, after all, James Blackford Penn the Fifth, no matter who his mother was, even if James' marriage had caused a certain reserve to come into the relationship between father and son.

William Beauchamp had never liked the Penns. They bought their groceries from a store in Richmond, delivered to them twice a week. Once, it had gotten back to William's father that Blackie, the third James Blackford Penn, had referred to him as "that ferret-faced little grocery boy." He stated his intention to shoot Blackie Penn, but was dissuaded without too much exertion on the part of his friends.

Three months before the wedding, in April of 1939, William told Jenny that Jimmy would have to change his name. It had bothered him for some time, although he had not before then mentioned it. But the idea of a child he was expected to rear carrying the name of James Blackford Penn the Fifth was more than should be borne, he felt.

Perhaps he wouldn't have been so adamant if he and Jimmy had gotten along better. But William Beauchamp was a bachelor who had never spent much time with four-year-old boys, and it seemed to him that this one must be worse than most. Jimmy whined too much, and it was his opinion that the boy had been spoiled. And part of being spoiled was being allowed to go around flaunting a name like James Blackford Penn the Fifth.

Jenny was 22. She already had lost much of her good looks, and a combination of depression and the starchy food on the O'Neil table had led to her gaining five more pounds since leaving Penn's Castle. She did not feel the tingle for William Beauchamp that she had for James Penn; she had not yet let him do much more than kiss her, and she awaited her wedding night with some anxiety.

Jenny had lost her confidence, the belief she had blithely worn so recently like a protective layer of skin, that life would be good to her. She knew (and if she didn't know, her mother and father were there to remind her) that William Beauchamp well might be her best remaining opportunity. To refuse to change Jimmy's name would be to refuse William, and refusing William was a gamble she was unwilling to take.

On May 15, 1938, James Blackford Penn the Fifth became James O'Neil Beauchamp. And it was decided, by William, that he would be called Neil.

The boy was first confused, then angry. He soon determined that the isolation from his father stemmed from this new name, which deprived him of toys and cake and long afternoons in a house far removed from either the O'Neils' farm or the new, no-nonsense, two-rooms-up, two-rooms-down dwelling William had built that year for his new wife.

"Not Neil! Not Neil!" he would scream. "Jimmy! Not Neil!"

It would make William furious, and he beat the boy for the first time two weeks before the wedding. He took him for a walk, just the two of them. Jenny, following orders, waited back at the house into which she soon would be moving.

They went out the kitchen door into the dirt and discarded lumber behind the house, then across Back Street and down a little path into the woods. William did not hold his hand as his mother did. Instead, he put the boy in front of him and more or less herded him down the path until they came to a tulip tree stump. There, William told him to sit.

Three times he ordered him to say his name was Neil. Three times the boy refused, after which William Beauchamp broke a switch from a forsythia bush, grabbed the child by the collar and hit him on the rump and legs with it until he was forced, through his tears, to give up his name.

It was not the end of the rebellion; there were other skirmishes. When Neil Beauchamp started school two years later, the teacher came by late in the afternoon of the first day and told William and Jenny that their son refused to answer to his name, insisted that he was Jimmy Penn, James Blackford Penn the Fifth, to be exact.

William wanted to beat him again, had already taken his belt off, but Jenny, four months pregnant with Millie, prevailed. She took her son into the bedroom and spent half an hour explaining to him that he must, once and for all time, understand that he was the son of William Beauchamp, not James Penn.

"Don't you think your daddy would have come and got you if he wanted you?" she asked the boy. "He's got all that money. Him and his lawyers could just come down here and take you away from me if he wanted to."

And she told him, because she thought he was old enough by then, that it made things hard on her when he refused to accept William Beauchamp's name along with his roof and food.

"Can't you do it for Momma?" she asked him. "Please?"

That was the last time Neil Beauchamp told anyone he was a Penn, but he still believed, deep in his heart, that his father would come and get him one day. Even after James and Virginia had Blanchard, when Neil was five, he never gave up.

Millie was born in 1942, Willamina two years later. Neil's memories of his days at William Beauchamp's are mostly of rocking bassinets, changing diapers and sharing a room with one or both of his little half-sisters. Only when Tom was born in 1947 did the Beauchamps add two more bedrooms.

About the same time he started school, Neil began his apprenticeship. Beauchamp's was a general store, selling groceries on one side, building materials on the other. Neil's first jobs were sweeping and cleaning, then stocking shelves and unloading trucks.

Visiting salesmen and townspeople remarked on how smart he was, in the older country sense of hard-working. William Beauchamp seemed hesitant to join in their praise, perhaps fearing that the boy would suffer a relapse and be the terror he had first encountered. He bragged to his friends, sometimes within Neil's earshot, that he had "straightened that one out."

Neil doesn't know how it came to be that way (and he never much considered such aspects of his young life until he had two years in prison to study the past), but he knew, even at 6 and 7, that to whine and cry and outwardly rebel would be an admission of defeat. He knew, even before he ever touched a baseball, that his day would come. And he quickly came to see that, for all William's boasting about his skills as a disciplinarian, it bothered his stepfather when he worked like a demon, day after day, never giving William the satisfaction of a tear or even a complaint.

The first time Neil hit a baseball, he was 8.

At that age, he was allowed to go outside and play with the neighborhood boys after he was through in the store, if Millie didn't need tending to.

The children on Dropshaft, along Back Street and up on Castle Road, were of such a number that the boys usually divided themselves naturally into two groups, the younger ones playing kick-ball or tag or other games they invented using the big trees in their backyards for bases. The older boys, from around 10 years old until they reached 14 or so, when serious work and other distractions took them away, played baseball from March until sometime in September when, by general agreement, the football was brought out. From late November until the last snow melted, they played outdoor basketball some days, football others.

They played in a cleared spot across the railroad tracks from Penn Presbyterian Church, in a flat, bare expanse that offered them, besides the field itself, one chicken-wire back-stop and a wooden basketball backboard with a rusted rim and occasionally a net. The baseballs they used were usually taped, having long lost their outer hides. Some of the players had gloves.

No one knew how a boy moved from the tag-players to baseball. Perhaps an older boy would promise to be there and then be seen, instead, walking beyond the field into the woods with a girl his age. Either a young boy of promise or one who was simply there would be allowed to play, right field usually. If the boy did passably well, or the older ones instinctively sensed that he belonged with them, he would be encouraged to stay around and play again. It might be two years before he could count on being an everyday player, one of those who decided who played and who didn't, one of the ones who got to be on the town team that sometimes would play contemporaries from West Creek or Mosby Forks.

Since school ended, Neil Beauchamp had chosen to watch the older boys instead of joining the ones his age. He had played softball at recess and felt that here was something that could make him happy, something at which he could excel, if he had the chance.

On this day, with two outfielders lost to summer jobs, perhaps some of the older boys remembered that Neil could outrun most of the 10-year-olds, or maybe they noticed that he was as tall as some of them.

He heard one of them ask another, the big red-haired boy who always batted cleanup for one of the two teams, if "that little sack of shit over there" could play. He didn't hear what the redhead said, but the first boy walked a couple of steps toward him and said, "Hey. You wanna play?"

Some of the others complained, the ones who were already smoking, telling jokes Neil didn't understand but laughed at when he heard them from outside the circle because he knew he was supposed to.

"He's only eight. He's just a baby," he heard one of them say.

But they let him play even though he didn't own a glove. The next-best option was a boy a year older who sometimes played jump-rope with the girls.

He hit ninth, of course. He didn't get to bat until the third inning; until then, his only action was running in from right field to back up the first baseman on two ground-ball outs, trying to impress with his boundless desire.

By then, it was almost sunset. The games lasted, usually, until the failing light caused someone to lose a fly ball or get hit by a pitch. Neil knew he had only one at-bat coming.

They all moved in on him. The three outfielders were just a few steps back of the worn base paths. In the distance, he could hear the train whistle signifying the return of the rail line's one engine to its terminus.

"Awright, easy out," he heard someone say.

"Let him hit it," another fielder, a boy smoking a cigarette while he played an indifferent third base, called out.

"Like hell," the pitcher, a boy just out of eighth grade, responded. He wound up and threw the ball.

The first pitch that came Neil's way, the first ball thrown overhand toward him in a game, he swung at. He somehow knew he would hit it, and he did, hard enough that it went past the right and center fielders on the fly. They were too stunned to even chase it for a long second, and by the time the ball had been retrieved and relayed to the infield, Neil Beauchamp was sliding into third base, the way he had seen the bigger boys do it. He can still remember the first sweet sound of cheers from the handful of grown men who were watching.

He never missed a game after that, when William Beauchamp could spare him at the store. He didn't hit a triple every time, and he was 10 before one of his long fly balls reached the tracks for a home run, but he was better than many boys three years older. He had, beyond size and speed, the reflexes and eyesight that would carry him even after the more obvious physical skills began to break apart. He could see the individual stitches as the ball left the pitcher's hand; when time speeded up for the less talented, more excitable boys, it slowed down for Neil Beauchamp.

He never forgot anything he saw on a baseball field, never failed to practice what he was shown until he had honed it to near perfection. He was the student that he never would be in the classroom.

William did not care very much for baseball. He was forced to work in his father's store when he was younger than Neil, he told Jenny, and he could see no good coming from a boy wasting his life chasing a ball. Jenny interceded, though, and Neil was allowed to earn enough money at the store to buy a fielder's glove and a bat by the time the next spring came around.

The glove he rubbed with neat's-foot oil every year. But it was the bat that he really wanted, even though it was less essential, since there was always at least one bat available, usually taped up and chipped at various places along its grained surface.

But Neil knew, even at eight, that this was what he was meant to do — hit a baseball. He played the field well, but catching and throwing were not what made him special, and he knew this from the first time he struck a pitched ball.

He coveted the bat from the first time he saw it in the Sears and Roebuck catalogue the October after his first triple. He wanted it for Christmas, but he didn't get it until he had earned it at his stepfather's store in the cold predawn of January and February, rising even before William to get the wood stove going before he left for school.

The blond wood Louisville Slugger had Lou Gehrig's name etched in cursive script on it, and to Neil Beauchamp, it was the most beautiful thing he had ever seen. The day it arrived, he went outside and swung it for an hour, at nothing anyone could see, smashing imaginary pitches for line drives that kicked up the chalk along the first-base line.

For the two seasons he had the bat, Neil never let anyone else use it. He was normally a generous boy, sweet-natured toward Millie and then Willa and later little Tom, but he was more than willing to fight anyone who wanted to use his bat.

Neil was a natural athlete, agreed all the 4-Fs and old men who brought crates and chairs across the tracks to drink from paper bags and watch the kids play, remembering themselves. "Natural athlete" was an arbitrary designation to them, like genius. Neil grew up thinking that a certain, small number of people were graced physically, another small number mentally. It was something you were born with, like brown hair or blue eyes, and although he was never allowed to even say the name, he attributed this gift to his Penn-ness. The fact that no Penn in memory had succeeded as an athlete made no difference. The Penns were tall and lanky, like him. He was a Penn. Thus, he believed he was bound for greatness.

He excelled in football, too, and in the desultory, sporadic basketball games. It seemed clear, though, that Neil Beauchamp was born to play baseball.

He listened to the Senators on the radio, when there were no chores to do, no little half-siblings to mind.

The boy won his precious hours at the field beyond the tracks by doing whatever his stepfather ordered done, never letting his anger show, as cool in the sight-lines of William Beauchamp's spite as he was in the batter's box. He seldom had to beg permission, though, because the other boys soon were coming around to beg it for him, even offering to do his chores.

"He's going to get big-headed," William would tell Jenny, after a platoon of boys older than his stepson had unloaded a truck of supplies in 10 minutes on Neil's behalf. "First thing you know, I'll have to take him down a notch."

Jenny, with a two-year-old and a new baby in tow, didn't even bother to argue. She seldom did. Neil generally felt loved by his mother, even if she didn't always show it. His memories of her now, more than half a century later, are of a young woman distracted and overtaxed, too busy with two and then three young children, too unsure of herself, to be his champion.

Neil Beauchamp at 10 was a boy of average looks. He would have profited from braces, and his ears grew at an alarming angle from his head. His hair was given to cowlicks. His eyes, a dark blue, were his best feature.

He was no scholar. His superiority in athletics did not carry past the classroom door. He had been no better than an average student before he and baseball discovered each other. Afterward, he was a clock-watcher, willing classes and days and years of school to go away and let him do what he did best.

Once, when Neil was in his prime, he and Kate visited Penns Castle for a week in the offseason. On the way home, Kate asked him why few of his mother's old stories seemed to involve him.

"I was working," he told her, "or playing ball." He didn't admit that he sometimes wondered, too. Sometimes, growing up, he feared that his mother wanted to forget James Penn and everything reminiscent of him almost as much as William Beauchamp did.

Tom shows Neil and David around the hardware store, now expanded as much as it can at its present location, spilling its fall flowers and wooden lawn furniture, its bird feeders and whiskey-barrel planters, onto the sidewalk and out the sides. He's been out of the grocery business for many years, and the immigrants from the city are providing him with a good living. This Tuesday, several women in their 30s and 40s are wandering the aisles, shopping for curtain rods, fertilizer and garden hoses. A few of the husbands are there as well.

"They come in here to buy a toggle bolt and wind up with ninety dollars of tools," Tom tells Neil and David out of the corner of his mouth. "Where the hell do people get all this money from?"

He leaves the store in the hands of his assistant manager, and the three of them walk over to the Station for lunch. Inside, there are murals of old locomotives on the walls. A bar area in the middle of the large room has been made over to roughly resemble a Pullman car, with stools alongside.

Tom seems to know everyone, new and old. A couple of men in their 60s, both classmates of Neil whom he can barely remember, stop to say hello. They try to talk a little baseball, but they obviously know more about this year's World Series and next year's chances than Neil does. He worries that they will think he's standoffish, but he's never been crazy about talking baseball.

He hears his name spoken, and out of the corner of his eye he sees a table of younger men, in dress shirts and ties, sharing a table perhaps 20 feet away, looking toward him. They look down as he turns to face them, and two of them laugh at something the other must have said.

Neil is used to this. There weren't many celebrities at Mundy.

SEVEN

NEIL SAYS THEY have a grocery list, that they have to go and check on David's car. Tom promises they'll be back at the store by 3 o'clock at the latest.

So they squeeze into the cab of Tom's truck, faded to near-pink and dwarfed by the newer one.

They turn left on Castle Road, away from Blanchard's, then left again on a street that was only a pair of ruts through the hardwoods the last time Neil saw it. They loop gradually to the right and soon are in sight of two long lines of brick homes, Georgian and Colonial mostly, flanking the road.

The leaves are nearly gone, so that Lake Pride is visible across three-quarter-acre lots, sending the low-riding sunlight to them on one hop. Cul-de-sacs peel off through the forest, most of them still works in progress, with finished houses next to bare footings. Some of the streets are not paved yet. The asphalt is cracked already and streaked red from the big trucks that rumble past, bringing lumber, taking away felled trees.

They go halfway around the lake and then Tom takes a left and they are on a road that circles Lake Pride Estates' other main selling point: the golf course. Twice the road crosses the cart path. Through the backyards, they can see occasional gumdrop bursts of brightly-colored sweaters as retirees ride alongside the emerald grass, casting long shadows as they get in one more Indian-summer round.

"Isn't this something?" Tom asks. "There's five hundred houses already built, and they say they plan to build a couple of thousand more. 'Course, the ones on the golf course got gobbled up fast."

"So I guess we can't go fishing?" David says, showing the twisted smile again.

"Nah. Not here anyways. I'd like to see somebody go traipsing through one of these folks' yards and throw a line in the water. Have your ass put in jail."

He points out one particularly large home, set on a small rise so that the golf course and lake are visible.

"They say that one's worth $600,000. How do you make that kind of money? You know, I watch 'em when they come in the store sometimes, trying to figure out what makes them special. I mean, I expect a man that lives in a $600,000 house to be Einstein or something, but some of these folks, I don't know if they can screw in a lightbulb or not."

Neil allows that he doesn't know much about how money flows. He's been the conduit for enough of it, God knows, but the mystery of how it went from some big-league team to banks and creditors and business partners and bartenders, some even to Tom and his sisters back in Penns Castle, Virginia, is something of a blur.

Neil knows that Tom has always wanted money, is actually making some now, it seems. He wonders if it's better to have it in ample supply and then lose it, or to go wanting for 50 years and then cash in, too old to enjoy it to the fullest, maybe, but old enough not to piss it away.

When he was in his prime, Neil thought money was what you chased if you didn't have a Talent. Now, without either, he can see that it has its uses.

Tom takes them up by the new strip mall back out on Castle Road, parallel to the golf course but not visible from it. The pizza parlor, Chinese restaurant, tanning salon, drugstore, and assorted shops offering golf equipment, movie rentals, antiques, "Christian literature" and women's clothing are identified by look-alike green signs beneath a common roof meant to imply Williamsburg.

Beside the strip mall sit an eight-theater movie complex and a grocery store. Tom parks, and the three of them go inside to do the one task Blanchard has assigned them.

It takes them almost an hour to find the dozen items on the list, mainly because Tom keeps running into people he knows, including two who recognize Neil and carry on short, strained conversations.

On the way back to Blanchard's car, the sun is low enough that Tom pulls his visor over the side window. With no warning, the deer crashes out of the brush 20 yards in front of them and runs off toward the golf course, in and out of sight in no more than two seconds.

"Jesus," David says.

"Dasher," Tom replies. "Damn deer is going to get somebody killed."

The deer around Penns Castle have gone full cycle since his youth, it seems to Neil. He never saw a live one when he was a boy, growing up in the town and walking to work or play through the then-untouched forest that surrounded it. Only after he left for baseball did they start coming back, and then, according to his sisters and Tom, they suddenly were everywhere, eating shrubbery all the way up to the houses, running in front of hapless drivers.

And now, according to Tom, they're gone again. It is possible that only the one remains, the rest thinned to nothing by cars and guns and real-estate developers. At least, no one has seen another live one this season. Two doe have been killed by cars since summer on Castle Road, plus many more on the state highway, and hunters have dispatched several south of the lake.

"People used to kill 'em for the meat," Tom says. "I don't know if these boys now would know what venison tastes like."

They drive back to the middle of Penns Castle and get out of the truck. The commuters from Richmond already are starting to stream by on Dropshaft Road in their white Cherokees and gray Lexuses that are even newer than their homes. The three of them lean against the metal and talk, David listening mostly. The wind has died down, and it's at least 60 degrees. It is, they all seem to silently agree, a good day to lean against an old red truck, breathe the late-fall air, and talk.

David drops his father and the groceries at the castle and drives back out to check on the car. The one bag Neil carries has black plastic handles, and David catches sight of the Virginia Rail in the rear-view mirror, his back bent slightly, a shuffle to his walk, carrying his load like an overburdened child or a very old man.

Neil sets the bag down and is about to knock when he sees that one of the two massive oak front doors is slightly ajar.

Inside, he finds Blanchard sitting to the rear of the great hall, not even aware that he's there, staring into the garden.

He scrapes his feet over the stone so as not to startle her.

"Oh, you're back already," she says, shaking her head as if to clear it. "What time is it?"

"Four o'clock."

"Four. . . It isn't." She looks at her watch. "Sometimes," she says, "I just kind of lose track."

He takes the groceries into the kitchen, which is far too small for such a house. When Blanchard comes in behind him, he finds that he is suddenly close enough to smell her perfume. He got a scent of it last night, and it jostled something in his mind. Now, he knows it is the same kind she wore when she was just a girl, too sweet-smelling, too devoid of nuance to be worn at this time, by a woman her age.

"I've missed you," she says, putting a hand on his shoulder and pulling him slightly earthward, so that their foreheads are touching. Neil looks down and remembers how small her feet were then, are now.

"We'd better put this away," he says. "Don't want the milk to go bad."

"Fuck the milk."

He takes her hand away and moves back half a step.

"Blanchard."

She takes a deep breath.

"Yeah. Yeah, OK. I'm fine." She waves an arm out toward him as if to push herself away, then goes back into the hall.

Her voice comes to him filtered through the thick wall. "It's just that I've missed you, is all."

He says nothing. After he puts the few groceries away, he follows her. She is standing by the back door, looking out at the same spot she was fixed on when Neil came in.

"Where do you think that dog went?" he hears her say, barely audible to him five feet behind her. "Where's old Cully, Neil?"

He puts his hand on her shoulder this time, and she leans to one side, trapping his fingers with her head.

Cully was her dog. Everyone in Penns Castle knew that. Blanchard Virginia Penn was born in 1940, and her brother two years afterward. They named him James Blackford Penn the Fifth, the name being vacant again.

Blanchard was fair with blue eyes, a beauty right from the start. Jimmy had dark hair and brown eyes that almost ran to black. They were so different in coloring that photographers had trouble doing both of them justice in the same picture. If Blanchard was just right, Jimmy was a shadow. It Jimmy was perfect, his sister looked washed out.

Blanchard was given the beagle puppy for her fifth birthday, much too young for such a responsibility, her mother claimed, but James Penn insisted that his golden daughter was ready for a dog. Besides, they still had a butler and a maid to deal with the realities of paper-training and do the bulk of the feeding and exercising.

But James Penn did expect Blanchard to walk the dog occasionally. She had named him Cully. Why Cully, her mother asked her. "Because Cully is a pretty name," she responded, brightly and without hesitation, and that was that.

Jimmy was three. Neil would see them on occasion, out in the yard when he walked past. Sometimes, he hid in the woods behind where the garden is now and watched as they played together, usually with the maid present to make sure they minded their parents' warning about staying away from the mineshaft openings.

The summer of 1945, soon after Blanchard got the beagle, Neil walked through the woods one hot, still July morning when not enough boys were available for baseball and his stepfather had no specific task for him for a couple of hours. He came up from behind the castle and was hiding deep in the greenery, some 30 feet beyond the pines that bordered the yard, watching. Before he had time to react, the puppy spied him, or smelled him, and made a mad dash directly for the Y-shaped oak in whose gap he rested, his feet nearly touching the ground. Before he could turn and run without being seen, Cully was nipping at his jeans, with Blanchard right behind, calling him. It must have been the maid's day off.

Blanchard stopped short when she saw the older boy there in the woods, half-turned away but too proud to run from a five-year-old. "Who are you?" she demanded, shading her eyes and looking up at Neil fearlessly.

"I'm your brother." He didn't know why he said it. Many people in Penns Castle had already forgotten that he was once James Penn's son, and certainly his 10-year-old peers were not aware of it. But he had always felt more Penn than Beauchamp, and it just slipped out.

"Nuh-uh," Blanchard said, shaking her head so violently that her pigtails whipped her face. "Nuh-uh. He's my brother," and she pointed toward Jimmy, playing in the dirt across the yard from them, oblivious to Neil.

"Well," Neil said, "I'm your secret brother. You can't tell anybody about me. Promise?"

Why he should have expected a five-year-old to promise anything, let alone keep it, he didn't know, then or later. But she did, even crossing her heart the way she had seen older children do it.

Neil slipped back into the woods, stopping once to chase Cully back toward Blanchard's cries, and he was gone.

He seemed, she would tell him years later, like a ghost, or some character from her storybooks.

The accident happened on a Friday, that same month, just before dark.

The war was all in the Pacific by then, and the adults were listening to the news on the radio. James and Virginia, Virginia's sister and her husband were on the added-on back porch, facing east, while the old butler made strawberry ice cream, working the hand crank as he leaned forward in his chair just around the corner.

Blanchard, Jimmy and Cully were playing with a rubber ball, and no one even knew where James Penn had conjured up such a treasure; rubber was like gold then. Blanchard would never forget its lime-green color or the shininess of it. The ball seemed to glow when she and her brother chased it in the twilight.

The children were too excited to sit still and wait for the ice cream to freeze. The adults had been drinking Virginia bourbon since before dinner, and no one noticed when Cully raced around the other side of the house, the children in pursuit.

Jimmy was wilder than his sister, you could see that already, everyone agreed. Blanchard had a mind of her own, they said, but she was a sensible child.

Jimmy was different.

One day when he was not yet three, they had to get him down from a pecan tree, from a branch eight feet off the ground. He had climbed onto the running board of his father's Ford, from there to the hood and thence to the roof, which offered him easy avenue to a notch in the tree.

He wasn't crying to get down when they came to rescue him. He was upset because he could go no higher.

"He's going to be an overachiever, always reaching," James Penn said optimistically.

Blanchard has tried all her life, with the help of psychiatrists and hypnotists, on quiet beaches and for many a black, sleepless night, to remember exactly how it happened.

She can remember the way that sloshing ice and water and rock salt sounded as the old black man turned the crank, can remember the quality of the waning light, the smell of the pork that had been grilled outside for their guests, the exact shade of green of the bouncing ball, the slightly-drunk laughter behind her as they ran into the front yard unnoticed.

Except for approximately two seconds, she can remember everything. Too much, really.

Her last psychiatrist, and the others, said she was blocking it, that she wouldn't let herself remember.

She knows they're probably right. Who wouldn't want to block those two seconds? The problem is, she remembers the rest.

It was such a long way from the front of Penn's Castle to the road that the children were unlikely to wander there, even if they hadn't been warned a thousand times.

This day, though, they were following Cully, who was working on a scent.

The beagle already had been given a whiff and a taste of rabbit, for James Penn did intend that Cully might be, in addition to a pet, a voice baying in distant woods as the light faded. James didn't hunt much, but he wouldn't have minded listening to a beagle work. The sound was as sweet to him as the chase itself was to Cully. He thought he might get another beagle soon, so the two of them could run rabbits together, a call-and-respose to welcome the night. That one could be Jimmy's.

Cully was tracking (or trying to) some rabbit that had recently been so arrogant as to wander through the now-wet grass at the foot of Penn's Castle.

He snuffled and barked in an exploratory way, unused to his newly-found hunting voice, zigzagging west, the children following.

Blanchard remembers them standing there, not 10 feet now from Castle Road. Jimmy had the green ball, and while Blanchard watched Cully work the ditch, nose down, he threw it more at her than to her. She had to chase the green sphere deep into the boxwoods, her brother giggling to her rear.

She doesn't think she was angry. She doesn't remember being angry with Jimmy ever, not really.

But somehow, the ball got thrown back, and somehow its trajectory carried it to Jimmy's left and beyond him. He turned around to chase it with his usual abandon. He only had one speed, his mother said. He had once knocked himself silly running head-on into the pump house chasing a blue butterfly.

Blanchard thinks she remembers the brakes squealing and then the barely discernible thump, but she isn't even sure about that. She recalls, clearer than the kitchen she just left, the lumber truck stopped in the middle of Castle Road, the raw smell of the wood and the big chains shackling it to the bed. She remembers the driver getting out and running over to the ditch, where he soon was joined by Cully. She remembers the driver turning away, how he looked.

She remembers running back toward the house, and seeing the adults already coming her way, walking and then running when they saw her face.

"I think Jimmy's hurt," is what she said, and then they all ran past her, toward the road.

They gave Cully away two neglectful weeks later. During that time, the only Penn who tried to show him any attention was Blanchard, but the dog seemed different, and soon she quit trying, too. The day James Penn took him away, she didn't come out of her room, and nobody spoke of Cully again for a long time.

Wat and Millie live near the intersection of Dropshaft and Castle. Except for trees and hills, they could see both the castle and Tom's house from their front porch.

Their oldest son, Ray, has come to dinner, too, along with his wife Patti and their daughter, Rae Dawn. Tom has walked over from his house beside the store. And Willa and her husband, Jack Stoner, a proctologist in Richmond, have come out as well. When Blanchard, Neil and David arrive, it's already dark, and the men are around back, where Wat has built a horseshoe pit.

The car was not ready when David got to the shop. He wished that he had had someone with him who spoke the language, someone who knew these people. He should have taken The Rail.

The one mechanic — not the morning one; he'd already departed — did not appear especially concerned that the car seemed not to want to run, "something electrical, I expect," and the best David could extract was the belief that they could get it started tomorrow morning.

David thought of doing something, a hair placed across the door like James Bond, maybe, so that he could tell, tomorrow, if the car has actually been touched by human hand when he comes back to get it.

"Well," he said, feeling totally impotent, "please do the best you can. I have to get back tomorrow night." The mechanic didn't even acknowledge him.

David is reintroduced to Willa and Jack; he meets Ray and his family for the first time, the big-haired blonde Patti and two-year-old Rae Dawn, a miniature of her mother. Ray is a heavyset 21-year-old who works for Philip Morris and, like Patti, is showing his loyalty by lighting up every 10 minutes.

They all listen with varying degrees of sympathy as David tells them about his deer-ravaged car.

"Is Dasher hurt?" Rae Dawn suddenly, solemnly asks her mother. This the most complete sentence anyone has heard the child speak, and the adults laugh, then strive to assure her that David's car is in much worse shape than the deer.

"Not much doubt about that," David mutters.

David believes there is an inverse relationship between cholesterol and latitude:

If a person were to leave the Washington suburbs driving south on Interstate 95, then veer off on Interstate 85 at Petersburg, following that road southwest, beyond Atlanta, eventually taking another road south through Alabama and a last one west through Mississippi, and if that person stopped for meals three times a day, taking pot luck, each day's meals would be larger than the previous day's until the unfortunate soul either exploded or reached New Orleans.

Even this far south is sometimes too much for him. At Wat and Millie's, he is offered ham and fried chicken, peas, beans and corn (all cooked with pork fat), white rice and gravy, mashed potatoes, biscuits and griddle cornbread, apple pie and two kinds of cake. There are multiples of every dish, and he feels that he is insulting Millie by not taking one helping of each.

He looks across the table and sees Neil eating in that squared-away fashion, head down, unable to slow even to the pace of the rest of the family, none of whom are chewing anything more than three times before swallowing. He spears a piece of ham with his fork, looks at it for a brief instant, and then pushes it rapidly into his mouth.

"Well, Neil," Willa says, "I guess this is the best food you've had in some time."

There is a slight hesitation in the smooth rhythm of the table. Before Neil can answer, Blanchard says, "Oh, I don't know, Willa. He had a pretty good dinner last night, too."

"Oh, I'm sure he did. I just meant, you know before that." Neil clears his throat.

"This is all very good," he says. "And you're right, Willa. I surely haven't had anything in the past two years as good as what I've had the last two nights. I'm afraid I'm going to get fat again."

"Oh, you never were fat," Millie says. "I bet you never weighed 200 pounds a day of your life."

After dinner, they talk for a while in the smoky, overheated living room.

Neil is glad to see Millie and Willa and Tom all doing so well, possessing a happy plenitude of paid-for homes, new cars, thriving businesses, children and grandchildren (or at least, in Tom's case, a comfortable lover), even as he feels the unease he spreads by his presence. He wonders how often he will visit the Beauchamps, and especially his half-sisters, if he becomes a permanent part of Penns Castle.

Growing up, he felt like another parent to them, getting them ready for school, fighting their fights for them. The resentment he felt toward William Beauchamp, before and after his stepfather's disappearance, he never transferred to the three of them. He has helped them — the careless loan here and there, the gift when he could afford it — but no more, he's sure, than they might have done for him.

But he doubts he will ever be a regular part of this family again. He wonders if he can fit into this town he thought he had outgrown so long ago, where it is understood that if one has the arrogance to leave for the bigger world, signifying that this one is too small, he can only properly come back wearing the winner's laurels. He is not really permitted the luxury of failure.

It's strange to him that Tom, who was only five when Neil left to play baseball, the one he feels he most abandoned, seems to be the one who does not reprove him with the barely-seen glance, the silenced conversation when he comes into a room. This he saw even before he went to prison. It's only worse now. But where else was he to go?

He excuses himself and walks outside to get away from the heat and noise. Jack Stoner is there, looking up into the clear November sky. Neil has not seen such stars, he realizes, in a long time.

"Can you believe how much they smoke?" Stoner asks. The only doctor in the family, perhaps he feels duty-bound, Neil thinks. "Don't they worry about the little girl?"

Neil says that he must have breathed a truckload of William Beauchamp's second-hand smoke. Jack shakes his head and notes that Millie has told him she has the early stages of emphysema.

"Well," Neil says, "think how bad it would have been if he'd stayed until she got out of high school."

Jack looks at him as if he wants to ask a question, seems to drop it, then charges ahead, asking anyhow.

"What did you come back here for?" he blurts out. "I mean, I know it's your home and all, but why here? I mean, if it had been me. . . ."

If it had been you, Neil thinks, you might have had a little money saved, might have been able to hang on to your wife, not lose touch with your son, keep a job. If it had been you, he wants to say, you wouldn't have done it in the first place; you'd have let them take her away, saved your butt and let the chips fall where they may.

He tells Jack Stoner, instead, about how the unexpected inheritance of half of Penn's Castle itself was about the only offer he'd heard of, either then or now.

Jack Stoner says nothing to this. In the dark, he looks like someone who is processing new, unexpected information.

"It might not be permanent," Neil says, thinking that this revelation will ease some minds.

EIGHT

"GODALMIGHTY, WHAT a piece of work those sisters of yours are," Blanchard says. "I swear to Christ, I thought I was going to have to hit Willa when she started talking about how DrugWorld is good for the economy. Like she wants Tim Rasher to go out of business."

Neil tries to calm her, but she seems to be feeding on her own fury, the anger growing steadily on the way back from Wat and Millie's.

"And then that Millie, she chimes in and backs her up. She and Wat go to church with the Rashers. And what's she going to do when Circuit City or somebody brings in some big-ass superstore and runs Wat out of business?"

Neil sits quietly, waiting for the storm to pass. He knows that neither Wat nor Millie want to see Rasher's Drug Store shut down, and they certainly don't want to see Wat's appliance store going head-to-head with a big chain. But he knows, and Blanchard will know as soon as she calms down, that Millie is bound to defend her sister.

He finds it strange that his allegiance has always seemed more naturally to flow toward Blanchard, the one half-sibling he didn't have to half-raise.

But it has always been this way.

Virginia could have no more children; there would be no more James Penns. "The buck stops here," his father would say in the years that followed, after too many drinks at the Commonwealth Club, and old friends and acquaintances would try to change the subject.

To compound the loss, Blanchard did not get over it, the way the doctors said she would.

Maybe the occasional odd act, the precursor of her zones, was already there and no one had noticed. Maybe she was walking some invisible tightrope and needed only the gust of senseless death to unbalance her. Maybe it would've been different if James and Virginia had been able to put it behind them, or fake it well enough to fool a bright five-year-old.

After the first endless night, no one ever asked Blanchard why they were playing so close to the road, why she didn't look after Jimmy better, how the ball came to bounce into Castle Road, right in front of a log truck in the dim Virginia woods.

But there was crying heard clearly through doors. There were conversations that ended when she walked into rooms. There were looks.

The first time Blanchard disappeared into one of her zones, at least in view of strangers, was the next year.

She started first grade that fall. Her parents sent her to the public school attended by all the children in the area. It had been James Penn's plan, before the accident, to enroll her in a private school in Richmond, but now they both wanted her nearby, out of their sight only when absolutely necessary. "We are trying," James told his mother, when she questioned their judgment, "to endure the unendurable."

Neil was in sixth grade. He knew Blanchard had started school; it was hard to miss, with Virginia driving up to the circular driveway every day and depositing the best-dressed child in that part of Mosby County.

Neil didn't speak to the little girl, but he kept an eye out.

Once, some third-graders appeared to be picking on her at recess, surrounding her in a threatening way as she stood next to the building watching the older girls jump rope. He cuffed one of them across the head and got sent to the principal's office for it.

One Tuesday in mid-November, while Neil and some of his friends were eating lunch, a scream brought all lesser sounds in the cafeteria to a halt. Actually, it was a series of screams, each the exact pitch and volume as the one before.

Blanchard Penn was standing in a corner of the large cinder block room, in full view of 200 children, and she looked as if she were trying to climb the gripless wall.

Two teachers were trying to calm her, but they seemed leery of coming within striking distance. The child was only six, but she did have a knife (albeit a rather dull one, suited for cutting overcooked pork and chicken) in her hand.

Neil got up from his seat and ran to where the teachers and curious grade-schoolers had her surrounded. In an act that owed nothing to rational thought, he walked past the inner-most line of gawkers, past the two teachers, and took the knife out of Blanchard's hand. The teachers closed in then, but Neil refused to leave the inner circle as they adjourned to the principal's office and tried to find out what had caused a bright first-grader to go temporarily insane. Their concern was only heightened by the realization that this particular first-grader's parents probably could have them fired.

Neil was her interpreter.

"She says somebody was trying to strangle her, that she couldn't breathe," he told the teachers and the principal who had swatted him with a Fly-Back paddle a month before.

Blanchard only nodded, then tried to make herself understood through more tears.

"Nobody was harming that child," one of the teachers said. Neil felt that even he, ranked in the bottom half of his fifth-grade class, knew more than this woman did.

"She just imagined it," he said in what he hoped was a

low-enough voice to the principal, a gray-haired woman who never had been seen to smile.

"No I DIDDUNT!" Blanchard screamed, wringing the fabric of her too-frilly dress with her hands, her face a bright pink. "I DIDDUNT!"

"No one answers," the secretary said. "Do we have Mr. Penn's number at work?"

"I can take her home," Neil said quietly. "I'm her brother."

The principal, in her second year at Penns Castle, started to deny this obviously false information when the secretary, a distant cousin of William Beauchamp, informed her that Neil was, more or less, telling the truth.

"No," the principal said, "you cannot walk this child home. You get back to class now."

She turned to Blanchard's teacher.

"We'll keep trying to reach Mr. Penn. In the meantime, we'll keep her in the office here, in case she has another attack."

"You stay here," she commanded Blanchard, then went back into her office, followed by the secretary, presumably to try to find the whereabouts of James or Virginia Penn. The first-grade teacher had to get back to her class.

Neil looked at Blanchard, who was calmer now but still seemed as if she were about to start crying again.

"Come on," he whispered, and the two of them were out the door, then out of the building, walking south, before the principal discovered to her horror that Blanchard was missing.

It took them 15 minutes to reach Penn's Castle on foot, taking a path Neil and his friends had hacked out and often used. By the time they got there, a deputy sheriff and the maid, who had been in the smokehouse fetching a ham when the first call was made, were standing outside next to a patrol car.

The maid's whoop of delight was followed by consternation when Neil and Blanchard walked up from their rear. Neil was given a stern lecture by the deputy and was taken back to school, where more punishment awaited.

Before Neil left the castle that day, though, James Penn, finally reached at his club, came screeching up. Virginia was visiting a sister in Baltimore.

"Where is she?" he demanded, his words only slightly slurred. and when he finally determined that she was safe inside, he started to go see about her. Then he noticed Neil.

"What are you doing here?" he said, disoriented.

"He said he was the girl's brother," the deputy told him.

Today, perhaps a little unhinged himself, he told the deputy, not even looking at Neil, "No. She doesn't have any brothers." And then he turned his back and went inside without another word.

"What I thought," the deputy said, taking Neil by the arm. "C'mon, son. Time to face the music."

On his return to school, Neil looked back at the house and saw Blanchard, in the moment before her father burst into her room to sweep her up, staring out the window at him.

"Your daddy was my guardian angel," Blanchard says now to David. In her version of the long-ago story, she is rescued because some older boys were picking on her. David looks to his father for confirmation, and Neil does not correct her.

The part about James Penn's final rejection of Neil, though, she tells honestly. She is capable, Neil knows, of telling sad truths about others. With herself, she does sometimes pull her punches.

In two years of enforced introspection, he has had to accept, among other hard realities, that part of him was drawn to Blanchard Penn out of some mystical link of blood and temperament, but that part of the pull was a desire to be a Penn.

He should have spit on everything Penn, the way William Beauchamp did, the way his mother did. But he didn't. He knows — and if he were to tell the story, this part could not be included — that he still yearned for James Penn to drive up one day, in a shiny, brand-new automobile, pick him up and carry him home. He can admit to himself that, after Jimmy Penn's death, he fantasized about stepping into the unquenchable void and somehow filling it, James Penn the Fifth redeemed by the loss, the prince again.

"Well, I guess your father must have felt bad about some of that, toward the end," David says.

"How so?" Blanchard asks, flipping a strand of hair out of her face, turning in his direction.

"I mean, to have left half this place to him and all."

Blanchard takes David's empty glass from his hand and goes into the kitchen.

"I guess," she says, above the tinkling of ice cubes, "that he finally thought he ought to for once do what was right."

Neil gets up to stretch. The arthritis has gotten worse, eliciting dim reminders of collisions with walls and second basemen and inside pitches. He needs to walk around, and he realizes as he's doing it that he is defining a rectangle about the size of his former cell.

"Besides," Blanchard says, coming back with two drinks so full that liquid spills down the sides with every slight tilt, "your father deserves a break. He's been looking after others long enough."

David wants to dispute this. He feels the old burn start inside him, fed by envy that the same Virginia Rail who was so absent in his life was capable of watching over others.

But instead he asks if Blanchard managed to spill any water at all in the bourbon.

"Not enough to hurt, honey."

Neil sits down again and takes another sip of his Coke.

"I mean," she says to David, "they had it rough after William left. That's when my father ought to have done something. If Neil hadn't been there, I don't know what would have happened to those girls, or Tom."

"Can we talk about something else?" Neil asks her.

David knows that his grandfather, or whatever William Beauchamp was, is a sore subject at family gatherings, a man who, when the going got tough, got going, as he heard Tom say once, long ago. He is so removed from Penns Castle lore, though, that he only knows the shorthand he's told himself and others for 20 years: The men of his family have a way of abandoning those close to them. He thinks of himself, when he considers this, the way a person might view his future if his ancestors had all died of the same, particularly vicious form of cancer.

"Tell me about William Beauchamp," David says. He knows he is being cruel.

Neil had always assumed that he would work for his stepfather until he was old enough to run away. At eight, this was his plan.

But then he started growing, and everyone recognized his talent with a bat and ball and glove. Suddenly, he saw a more defined way out, one that would not involve living wild in the woods. About the same time, he started to realize how much his mother and his little sisters depended on him, the upward, trusting looks Millie and Willa gave him — he might as well have been a parent — the small fingers wrapped around an older-brother's pinky.

Not long before his 13th birthday, though, Neil's dreams of running away from William Beauchamp were scotched for a very simple reason: William Beauchamp beat him to it.

His mother and stepfather had never had, in Neil's memory, the kind of romance he and Kate had in their early married years. He has always supposed that this was normal for the time and place. There was little poetry that he can recall in Penns Castle, circa 1945.

If their relationship took a turn for the worse, he cannot remember it. He just remembers being roused one late-fall day in 1947, well before dawn, even earlier than he usually awoke, by his mother's words: "He's gone."

Those were the exact words his aunt had used when she came up to their house, two years before, to tell Jenny that Gerald O'Neil had died in his sleep. Neil wondered for brief seconds if his sinful wish, almost a prayer, had been fulfilled.

The "gone" of William Beauchamp, though, was of a more mysterious nature. He did not die in his sleep, or in any other manner witnessed by Jenny or her family. He was, truly, gone. He left no note, either with his wife or their lawyer. He did not, to his credit, clean out the $546 they had managed to save.

For years, people would claim to see him, on a street in Richmond, on a visit to Baltimore or New York or Virginia Beach. He had siblings, one brother still in Penns Castle, and they claimed to be as baffled and uninformed as Jenny.

She had a four-month-old, a three-year-old and a five-year-old, in addition to Neil. They had the house, which William had labored greatly that fall to expand, as if to bestow one last gift on them. And they had the store, which Jenny could only see, in her present state, as a mixed blessing.

The night before, he had told Jenny that he would have to go back to the store and work on the inventory. He usually drafted Neil to help with this, and the boy was relieved to be excused, although being excused from work by William Beauchamp should have raised a warning flag. William said he might be at it most of the night.

When Jenny awoke at four a.m. to tend to the baby, the other side of the bed was still cold. After Tom's feeding, she put on a sweater and went next door, to find the store locked and dark.

She returned to the house, and that's when she looked in the closet and saw that the large suitcase was missing, along with several shirts and pairs of pants. It amazed her, when she had time to think on it, that a man with three children under the age of six, and a wife home and nursing, could have managed to spirit out even the lightest essentials for such a getaway.

He must have walked to the state road and caught the bus into Richmond, since the last train on the Penn and Richmond line went east in the late afternoon. From Richmond, he could have bought a ticket and gone in almost any direction. He was a man who could have lost himself easily in a crowd, all agreed. He was in all ways unremarkable.

They soon found small incongruities in the books at the store, enough to let a man traveling alone put several states between him and what he was escaping.

Once Jenny more or less accepted that William had not been kidnaped, had not fallen down a mineshaft or been stricken with amnesia, had indeed just left, she showed more steel than many of her neighbors thought she possessed.

She enlisted various family members to help take care of "the babies," and she and Neil tried to run a store. Neil was, once he had willingly given up the idea of regular school attendance, more capable than his mother, since he had worked there for an average of 30 hours a week since he was eight years old.

Blanchard would sometimes slip into town, always coming by the store to visit the strange dark-haired boy who called himself her brother. Sometimes, he would give her a piece of candy. Sometimes, he would assign her some light, harmless work.

One afternoon, Virginia found her there, separating the empty soft-drink bottles and putting them in the correct crates.

She took the girl by the arm, without a word, and half-led, half-dragged her out to the waiting car.

But Blanchard was willful, and she always returned.

Neil and Jenny went through a year like that, the two of them working 12-hour days and depending on the honesty of underpaid clerks for the rest. Finally, toward the end of 1948, Jenny called Neil into the store's little office one afternoon. With her was a tall, well-dressed and well-fed man whom she introduced as Wade Ramsey. He was a first cousin of Jenny's from Richmond. Neil had only seen him once before, at an O'Neil reunion.

The Ramseys were a little better off than the O'Neils had been; they had some money for capital ventures (although Jenny noted to herself that she had not heretofore been the beneficiary of any of their help). Wade Ramsey was offering to buy Beauchamp's, "lock, stock and barrel."

Neil was almost six feet tall, larger at 13 than his mother's cousin. It irritated him that the man did not choose to shake his hand, that he instead sat with his thumbs hitched on the inside of his belt and remarked on how much "the boy" had grown.

Neil listened as his mother explained that Wade Ramsey was offering them a certain sum of money, enough to enable Jenny to take care of her children. She might have time to do some part-time housekeeping for other women and bring in a few more dollars, without the store to tend.

Neil asked his mother if they could talk in private, and they went out behind the store, into the crate-strewn back yard.

He told his mother that he didn't want to give up the store, which surprised her, because she had always assumed that he despised it, saw it as an impediment between him and base-ball.

"What if we only sold him half the store?" Neil asked her. "What if I worked over there every afternoon, as much as he will, and we just sell him half?"

Neil had learned almost nothing from his stepfather. The one thing with which he can now positively credit William Beauchamp was the advice that had been given him (and probably not meant to be of any use) three years earlier. He and William had just finished a 12-hour Saturday. They were both exhausted, and his stepfather bought him a Coca-Cola, a rare show of camaraderie. As they sat there on two upturned boxes in the back of the store, William Beauchamp looked over at him, pointing a finger accusingly, as if he had read Neil's resentful mind.

"The reason we do this," he told his stepson, "is because it's ours. If you work like a dog all day, and you're just doing it for someone else, it ain't worth a damn. This is ours." And he jammed his index finger down hard on the wood.

By 1948, Neil had come to feel strongly that William Beauchamp was full of crap, a man who would walk out one night and never even glance back at his precious store or his family. But the advice struck a chord. He thought, as tired as he was some nights, that this was about all the Beauchamps were going to have, and they'd better hang on to it.

That was what he told his mother.

"How can we hold on to it?" she asked him. He told her they would go and see their lawyer, William Beauchamp's lawyer, and get him to write up something that would protect them.

Wade Ramsey took it better than Jenny thought he would, and he finally agreed, weeks later. He would, over the next several years, put less time into Beauchamp and Ramsey than Neil did, but he provided a lot of good advice and some valuable capital, and he and Neil got along better than either of them thought was possible. The post-war years were good for them, and they started edging more and more into the hardware business.

By the time Neil left home, Tom was five, and it was established that one-half of Beauchamp and Ramsey was in the hands of Jenny O'Neil Beauchamp and her children as long as they wanted it that way. By then, Jenny was able to work the hours that Neil had earlier labored, learning more about hardware than she could have believed possible. Neither of the girls saw the store as anything but a place to toil until they could leave home, and by the time Tom, as uninterested in school as Neil had been and half as athletic, turned 18, it was waiting there for him, and he was ready for it.

By then, too, Wade Ramsey was getting near retirement, and none of his children wanted to be in the hardware business in Penns Castle. Neil batted .314 and drove in an even 100 runs for the Indians that year, and part of his next-year's raise became the loan that turned Beauchamp and Ramsey into Beauchamp's again.

It is after midnight when Blanchard finishes.

David is wide awake half an hour after his normal bedtime. He wonders why he has never heard or even sought this story before. He knows he's as much to blame as his father is.

"How did you find time?" he asks, swallowing. "To play baseball and go to school, I mean."

"To go to school," Neil repeats. "Well, there wasn't much school. But the coaches looked after me. Didn't want me to drop out.

"And, you know, you're young. You've got all the energy in the world."

"All the energy in the world," Blanchard says, smiling. "You look like you might have done well to have saved some of it for your old age."

She grows solemn and looks at Neil closely, as if searching for something, then looks away.

"I'm sorry," she says, and the light reflects off the watery surface of her eyes.

There is nothing to talk about, Neil knows, certainly not at this late hour.

He gets up, stiffly, and he and David go down the long hallway to their bedrooms.

Inside, with the door closed, Neil looks in the mirror, something he has avoided doing very much. He has never been a vain man, but he is laid low by the lines, the horizontal ones across his brow and the deep vertical one that bisects it, and by the hair, almost snow-white.

How did this happen? he asks himself, staring. Where did the Virginia Rail go? When he went to prison, he was booze-heavy and red-faced, certainly, but he had energy. He had a sense, every day, that something might happen. The figure in the mirror seems drained, eviscerated.

He wonders, in the near-sleep he has achieved standing up, how a man can avoid his own reflection, through shavings and washings, for two years. He supposes that anything is possible if you want it badly enough.

NINE

THE SIGN RESTS on a giant golf ball and reads "Par-3." The letters and symbol are white on Day-Glo orange. Underneath, in smaller letters: "Baseball, Softball, Putting Greens, Refreshments." As they get closer, David sees the canvas-covered cages. On a whim, he whips the truck into the short exit lane and they climb a small hill to an almost-empty parking lot.

He questions the impulse. He is not a spontaneous person, not spontaneous enough, according to Carly. But something about the batting cages connects, and he knows before he thinks about it that this is a rare common point, a place where he and the Virginia Rail once intersected briefly.

Blanchard was out when they made their way to the dining room. While the two of them were preparing a breakfast of cold cereal, milk and orange juice, she came in, wearing jeans and an old shirt, both streaked and splattered with clay. She said she had been for a walk. She wanted to make them a hot breakfast, and when they insisted that they were fine, better fed than they had any right to be, she began crying, apologizing for not being there, apologizing for things that David couldn't even see.

He explained that they had to get a move on, because he wanted plenty of time to hound the mechanics at Garner's before he and Neil went to see the parole officer.

"I'm sorry," she said again, as they walked out the door. "I'm sorry," and they both felt guilty for not staying, but it would have been another hour off their day.

Then, the morning mechanic at Garner's was nowhere to be found. The shop was locked. After a few minutes of waiting, looking in the rear-view mirror every time a car passed on the highway, David walked over and peered through the window at his damaged car, locked in the little parking lot, abandoned as a stray puppy, untouched since the evening before.

Neil saw no reason to tell him that it was not unusual for an automobile mechanic in Penns Castle to take an unplanned day off when the late-November weather turned to Indian summer and deer season was in.

"We'll get it taken care of," he said to David when he came back to the truck. "It'll work out."

David smacked his left fist against the steering wheel.

"How did you stand this place? Growing up here, I mean."

"It didn't seem so bad then. I was part of it. I've changed, probably. It hasn't."

"It ought to."

"Well, Blanchard thinks it's changing too much."

David started the truck, then sat for a minute, afraid the mechanic would show up as soon as they left.

"What they need to bring in here is a garage," he said, "one that actually fixes things. It ought to put these low-life cocksuckers out of business in about five minutes."

Neil flinched, surprised at his own squeamishness. He'd spent many hours the last two years with men who were capable of using certain profanities as nouns, verbs, adjectives, adverbs, gerunds and infinitives, sometimes in the same sentence, and his life in the big leagues was spent among profane men who spit out streams of curse words and tobacco juice the way some men breathe.

But he never really grew accustomed to it.

He has always disliked the heavier, darker profanity. The players who used it the most, he felt, were the ones who had to, as if acting the part would raise their meager batting averages, keep their curve balls from hanging. And in prison, the loud, swearing ones were always looking over their shoulders, checking to see who they intimidated, and who they didn't, never at ease.

David saw his discomfort.

"What? You haven't heard worse than that lately? Where've you been?" He stopped short, letting the words hang in the air.

Now, on the way to the Virginia Rail's first meeting with his parole officer, they are sitting in the parking lot of what is advertised as a "fun center."

Two older women walk up the path to the small golf course's clubhouse on pale, heavy, varicose-veined legs. Only one baseball batting cage is in use. A father stands behind the screen, hands gripping the fencing, face pressed against it, feet out behind him a little. Inside, holding a metal bat and facing a Rube Goldberg contraption of a pitching machine, is a boy who might be eight or nine years old.

"Want to hit a few?" David asks.

There is nothing Neil would like to do less. He shakes his head.

"Come on. It'll be good for you. Do something you're good at."

In the cage, the boy swings at and misses two pitches in a row. The father makes an impatient movement to the side, as if he has an urge to rush into the cage and hit the ball himself, then say, "There. That's how you do it." But he stays behind the screen. The boy fouls one off, misses two more, then hits a dribbler that barely reaches the netting set up to stop balls 10 feet behind the pitching machine. From where Neil and David sit, it is hard to tell how fast the pitches are coming, or what exactly the father is saying, but it is obvious to both of them that his clapping after the one fair ball is more in sarcasm than praise.

"Let's go," Neil says. David doesn't move, though.

When the father and son are finished, the man walks two steps ahead of the boy on their way back to the big sports utility vehicle. They get in their respective doors, not looking at each other, and the truck squeals angrily out of the empty lot.

"Remember? . . ." David asks, then stops.

"No," Neil says.

But of course he does.

Neil Beauchamp was never quite sure how one went about rearing a male child. He has had ample time to consider it, and he wishes he could have had another chance.

One of his cellmates at Mundy was a ghost of a man who had spent much of his adult life as a sworn enemy of various governments. In the spring of 1995, he had broken into a restricted military installation in eastern Virginia, bent on doing as much damage as a 60-year-old black man armed with wire-cutters could do. He did manage to strike a guard, and he was serving a three-to-five-year sentence.

The man was left alone by most of the other prisoners, too old to be dangerous or to be meat for the sexual predators. He and Neil supposed they had been thrown together because of their age; they had nothing else in common. While Neil was batting his way into the baseball Hall of Fame, letting his manager, team traveling secretary, broker, business partners and wife deal with inconveniences such as hotel reservations, taxes, investments and child-rearing, Ambrose McDaniels was fighting. He was the first in his family to graduate from high school, then college, never attending an integrated class until law school.

He spent the '60s fighting state and local governments in his native Alabama, then, with Vietnam, took on a larger foe. He preached that black men and women were expected, and would be expected in the future, to fight America's wars, and he exhorted everyone of color to refuse to fight "whoever, whenever, whatever."

Neil did not agree with all that Ambrose McDaniels said, and they had arguments that were both amiable and predictable. What did strike Neil, though, was his cellmate's religion.

Neil knew almost nothing about reincarnation, and when it was first explained to him, his wonderment provoked McDaniels to ask him if he had spent his whole life in an isolation booth.

Neil, whose religion was not then and is not now a solid object, more of an occasional scented vapor than a rock, was intrigued by the concept. The more he thinks about it, the more he wishes for reincarnation, or something like it. He knows he could do better next time, especially as a father. He has learned something, he believes, but he wonders what good it does him now.

Plus, from what Ambrose McDaniels has told him, he fears his next appearance on Earth might be as one of the lesser invertebrates.

Back then, Neil might wake up one morning and realize that he was letting Kate and the neighborhood raise his son. It would be a fall or winter day, or a rare summer day when the Indians were home and playing at night, leaving at least some of the morning free.

The day he and David both remember, as they watch the little boy struggle to please his father with a line drive up the middle, was in mid-June, 1970.

That morning, Neil lay there for a few minutes with his eyes closed, waking up to the sound of the clothes dryer, to

Kate cleaning breakfast dishes down the hall, to the vague murmur of a faraway television.

It came to him, as sleep slowly lifted, that he had not acquitted himself very well the night before. He had gone hitless in three at-bats, suffering the still-rare indignity of being lifted for a pinch-hitter in the ninth inning of another losing cause.

The crowd had been so small that he could hear individual insults. One man in particular, one of the greasy-haired regulars who sat behind the dugout for the sole purpose of tormenting the unpromising home team, had been on him for several nights now. Neil's teammates, most of whom had felt his sting, called him the Polish Sausage, in honor of his ancestry, appearance and eating habits.

The man had never really bothered Neil. He had seen teammates run out of the major leagues because, when things went bad, they developed such rabbit ears that they could pick up insults half a stadium away.

That was not him, Neil assured himself, but then, he realized later, things had really never gone badly for him before, not on a baseball field. The kind of year Neil Beauchamp was headed for that year would have pleased most players. He would end the season at .287, with 14 home runs and 77 runs batted in. But Neil could see the diminishing returns he was getting at 35, and he could not imagine 36 being any better.

And so, the night before, there had been two voices in his ear.

The interior one whispered that it would soon be over, that before many more nights, he would reach the end of the only life he had really prepared for.

The exterior one was somewhat louder, with much the same message.

Over the past few games, the Sausage sometimes called him the Virginia Whale, in honor of the 20 pounds he had added over the past three seasons. Sometimes he was the Virginia Snail, after he had failed to reach a sharply hit ball down the first-base line, one he would have had two years earlier. Last night was the first time Neil could detect the occasional titter, an outright laugh now and then, from the Sausage's neighbors.

Neil knew the futility of answering the insults. The Sausage apparently spent much of his day thinking up torments for the Cleveland players. He was clever, and he never did anything in response to a threat or curse except laugh in the most perfect delight and stick the blade even deeper.

Neil knew this, but then he was called back from the on-deck circle, just as he was taking his first step toward home plate, focused on salvaging a dismal night. A kid of 22 passed him, pumped up, swinging two bats, determined not to be sent back to Buffalo.

"Hey, Whale," the Sausage screamed, and Neil could see him out of the corner of his eye, a yellow smudge of mustard on his chin. "Whale! Hey, Virginia Fail-ure!"

Neil allowed himself a quick glance up, and that only encouraged the man.

"Now batting fifth," he bellowed, using his program as a megaphone and doing a perfect imitation of the Cleveland announcer, "in place of the overpaid, underachieving Virginia Failure, who has been given the rest of the evening off to be with his family. . ."

Neil was on the dugout roof before he realized what he was doing, the bat still in his hand. He would always be grateful to the three teammates who dragged him back by the ankles.

The Polish Sausage would ease up on Neil after that, the only time anyone could remember the man showing any compassion, but in the silence Neil would feel a sympathy that was almost worse than the razzing.

After the game, Neil had gone out with the only Indians player older than himself, a relief pitcher getting by on a knuckleball, and had gotten as drunk as he ever did. Neil Beauchamp was not, in his playing days, a drinker. It bespoke, to him, an absence of the control that he felt he had over events.

This time, though, he had succumbed. Now, lying in bed, he wanted to repair things. And part of that repair, he thought, would be to "do something" with his son.

When he shambled into the breakfast nook, the sight of his backside, on the front sports page, as he was dragged off the top of the dugout and away from the seemingly shocked Polish Sausage, only made him more determined to right himself.

Kate did not speak to him, only patted him on the shoulder as she went past, on the way to get more eggs and bacon from the refrigerator. She was still defending him then.

Neil wandered into the family room, where David was lying on the floor, watching cartoons on television.

He sat down in the chair behind him, moving deliberately so as not to spook his son, who, it seemed to Neil, was on the jumpy side.

"Hey," he said after the two of them had watched in silence as a cartoon coyote went over a cliff and then, in a small poof! hit a canyon floor miles below. "How about if we go hit some balls?"

The pitching machines were new to their neighborhood that year, part of a complex that also offered miniature golf and trampolines.

For some time, Neil had meant (when he thought of it in an idle moment) to take David there. He knew, from the one Little League game of his son's that he'd seen and the other six he'd heard about, that David was not having a great season. He was a second baseman, usually batting seventh. Neil could tell, just from the two times he'd seen David bat, that his son was neither a power hitter nor a contact hitter. What David was, the best Neil could tell, was an occasional hitter. And his fielding did not seem prizeworthy, either. It crossed the Virginia Rail's mind that David might not be starting at all if his last name weren't Beauchamp.

David did not respond at first to his father's offer. When asked again, he said, "I guess so," and then got up without a word to change clothes and get a bat.

The complex was called, according to the large green sign that hovered above it, "Hit Something!" Most of the pitching machines already were in use, and it was necessary for David to squeeze in between two older boys who were knocking balls into the screen with grunts of satisfaction.

Neil was recognized almost immediately, even with sunglasses on. Most of the comments were sympathetic; this was, after all, his neighborhood, even if he seldom was seen in it except driving to and from the ballpark.

A small crowd of children and some parents gathered around him, asking for autographs, the adults offering insight into what was wrong with the Indians, telling him about their own sons who were tearing up one youth league or another.

At his father's command, David chose the highest of the three pitching speeds, which, it soon became apparent, was faster than anything he would face in a Little League game.

"You won't learn anything hitting powder-puff pitches," Neil told him. He instructed from behind the fence.

Move closer to the plate. Don't put your foot in the bucket. Choke up a little. Don't close your eyes, for God's sake.

It was inevitable that the audience would take all this in, and almost as inevitable that Neil would, without thinking about it, turn a morning with his son into a community batting practice lesson, with David as the "before" who could, with work, be turned into a hitter.

"Now, see there," Neil said, turning to the two older boys who had used all their quarters and now were watching David being overmatched by the pitching machine. "He's bailing out, putting his foot in the bucket. You've got to keep both feet in there, got to stay squared away toward the pitcher. . . . OK now, swing! See, he closed his eyes."

"Can't hit what you can't see," one of the older kids observed, and there was general agreement and a few laughs.

This went on for half an hour. Twice, David tried to leave, but Neil sent him back, putting more quarters into the slot, giving more free advice.

When it was over, Neil had provided a couple of dozen Chagrin Falls boys with a free batting lesson from a future Hall-of-Famer, which was what they already were calling him in the newspapers.

"You're lucky to have a dad like that," one adult said to David as he left the batting cage, finally permitted to quit. "You listen to him, and you'll be a good one, too."

Neil Beauchamp was not a quick study of humanity in those days, but even he realized he had lost sight of the morning's goal. David seemed to be striving mightily not to cry as they went back to the car.

Neil knows now what he only dimly perceived then: Almost none of the hard lessons he brought to adulthood seemed to be of any use to his more sensitive, less athletic son. Neil would have crawled over broken glass as a boy if someone had taken him aside for a rough but loving lesson in the finer points of baseball. By the time Neil was under the wing of an adult male who cared enough for such instruction, he already knew almost as much about baseball as his high school coach.

That day, driving back home, he tried to tell David that, but the man who was overmatched against the Polish Sausage was not much better with his own son.

Finally, he told David that they would go back again, early in the morning when no one else was there, just the two of them.

And then he had to rush inside to get ready for the long drive to the park.

They never went back to the pitching machines.

When they get to the parole office, they find that the appointment that had been arranged for Neil before he left Mundy has been postponed. Neil's parole officer has the flu, the unapologetic secretary tells them, and he won't be back again until the next Monday.

The two men leave. It's past lunchtime, and David pulls into a hamburger stand that has been given a '50s retro look, with much tile and neon. The patrons apparently are expected to eat in their cars, because there are no public doors, only small windows for ordering.

Small metal tables have been placed outside, and Neil asks if they can eat their burgers and fries there, in the open.

"You know," David tells him as Neil works away with speed and efficiency at the meal before him, elbows to the side, head down, "we're in no hurry."

Neil understands and tries to slow down, but before he even realizes it, he is eating almost as fast as before. He stops himself again.

"It's going to take awhile," he says. "I'm sorry."

David wipes his mouth with a napkin. It is strange to hear the Virginia Rail apologize for anything.

"It'll come back to you," he says.

On the six-lane boulevard in front of them, there is a squealing of brakes and a slight bump, an almost-delicate tinkling of glass. One car, stopped at a red light, has been pushed partly into the nearest intersection by a minivan. The car's driver stays behind the wheel while the other man gets out slowly, as if he's trying to remember the protocol or devise a plan for minimum loss.

David turns to watch. Within a minute, a police car arrives and an officer gets out to direct the already gridlocked lunch hour traffic at the intersection.

When David resumes eating, he sees that his father has spilled some of the soft drink he was holding. He looks pale, and old.

"That's why I don't like to drive just yet," Neil says.

"Don't worry. We'll get you back in the saddle soon enough. No hurry. You'll get the hang of that, too."

Neil nods in the affirmative, to be polite.

He barely saw the trooper that night. He remembers him more from the feel, the solid thump, harder than the deer, because the car caught him full on, the whole bottom half of his body absorbing the metal punishment.

He wouldn't know until later that the man had been killed on the spot. Lacy Haithcock was 24 years old, and he left behind his parents, his fiancée and two sisters. He had been all-region in football and wrestling, and he had asked nothing more from life than to be a Virginia state trooper.

"It was all he ever wanted to do," Lacy Haithcock's father had said at the sentencing hearing, looking at Neil Beauchamp when he said it.

When the judge had said five years, with three suspended, the Virginia Rail thought, despite the horror he felt at finally, suddenly arriving at the place to which he had seemed destined to land for 20 years, that this was only fair. Somebody ought to pay more than this for Lacy Haithcock's young, wasted life.

They throw their trash away and are back at the car when a middle-aged man approaches tentatively.

"Excuse me," he says, "but are you Neil Beauchamp?"

Neil nods yes, and the man shakes his hand.

"I used to follow you all the time, in Cleveland and Detroit," he says. "You were as good as any of 'em."

Neil thanks the man, who produces a mustard-smeared napkin and ballpoint pen. Neil writes his name, the letters bleeding into the soft paper.

The man thanks him, and Neil senses what's coming next. They always wait until they have the autograph, as if he wouldn't grant it otherwise.

"You can still pull yourself together, Rail," he says, Mr. Familiarity now, comfortable as a boyhood pal. "We've all had our share of screw-ups. Make us proud of you again."

Neil nods, saying nothing, as the man turns and walks away, a spring in his step, eager to tell his co-workers the priceless advice he gave Neil Beauchamp.

When he was in his prime, it amazed Neil that so many people thought they owned a piece of him. It was flattering in a way, when he was on top. Later, the same people seemed to feel somehow robbed, as if they had wasted all those cheers, all those days following the box scores, all that belief.

Before, their disappointment focused on things like diminishing productivity, divorce, booze and bankruptcy. What will it be like now? Maybe, he thinks, hopes, he's let everyone down so badly that they eventually will leave him alone.

TEN

THE CAR IS in a different spot when they return to Garner's. David can't believe how his heart leaps at such minor progress.

The morning mechanic apparently did not show at all, and the afternoon one has on the telltale camouflage pants of the deer hunter. There is a dark stain on the right leg just above the knee. He says the car is fixed. When David goes to start it, though, after charging almost $200 on his VISA card, it nearly catches the first time, then grows progressively weaker with each prayerful turn of the key and pat of the accelerator.

The mechanic, a young man barely out of his teens, opens the hood and looks inside with what seems depressingly like incomprehension.

"Come back around five," he says at last. "I think I know what's wrong with this thing. Damn Jap car." David wants to tell him that he has never had anything go wrong with a Japanese car in his 15 years of owning them that a competent mechanic couldn't fix in under an hour, but he fears he might never escape Penns Castle if he speaks his mind.

"That'll still give me time to get back home by eight," David says when he returns to the truck, and Neil nods.

No one seems to be home at the castle, but then, when they walk to the glass-paned doors at the back of the great room, they see Blanchard in the garden. She is wearing jeans and a burgundy silk blouse. She seems to be examining the remains of fall — a few mums, purple and gold, some geraniums and pansies still seeking precious heat in half-barrels along the side. The huge, thick stone walls flanking the plants catch the sun and block the wind, a gift of two extra weeks for Blanchard's garden.

In the dwindling light, her hair shines golden, and David is stirred by her figure as she bends over to pick one of the mums.

"That," he says to Neil, "is a fine-looking woman, even if she is my aunt."

"Half-aunt," Neil says. He is watching her, too.

Blanchard Penn wakes up some mornings and doesn't know where she is.

She likes the tingle she gets delaying the moment when her mind gains traction and it comes back to her. It is not unpleasant, not at all, to be lost. There are worse things.

Even in the middle of the day, she might stop after writing a letter and wonder for a moment what to put for a return address.

When the cancer finally took her father last year, and when his net worth was found to be somewhat less than she had imagined, so much less that something had to be sold, she put the West Avenue townhouse on the market and moved back to Penn's Castle.

People she knew in Richmond, including her lawyer, tried to talk her into staying in the city, wondering out loud what she would do with herself "out there." But she knew Neil Beauchamp, and she knew he would not be happy living a few feet from strangers, prying eyes everywhere. He had told her enough about prison that she knew what was best for him.

"There'll be enough to live on, after we sell the town-house," she assured Betsy Traywick, with whom she had lunch twice a month. "And it'll be good for Neil. It's half his, you know. He's my brother, and I'm going to see that he's looked after for as long as I can."

Blanchard's small handful of friends were more worried about her than they were about the homecoming prisoner she called her brother, but nobody really knew how to broach the subject. Blanchard could be so high-strung.

When she told Neil about his inheriting half of Penn's Castle, he was surprised. He had not spoken with James Blackford Penn since he left home, more than 40 years before.

"He was always sorry," Blanchard had said, holding his hands in the crowded visitors' room at Mundy, where the two of them were always surrounded by other prisoners, their families and the guards. "He wanted to make things right before he died."

Neil did not necessarily want to live in the old house with its memories. He had gotten prideful satisfaction out of it for some time, driving past on rare visits home and seeing it deteriorate, as much as something of solid English stone could. The process had started even before James and Virginia and their daughter abandoned it for Richmond in 1956.

Now, though, he supposed that he and Penn's Castle were a match for each other. The house, with Blanchard ploughing much of her remaining money into its revival, probably was holding up better than the Virginia Rail.

He acted grateful, even if the deed was in both their names. He didn't tell Blanchard how uneasy he was with it all, how he would have done otherwise if there had been an otherwise.

The young Blanchard Penn had several more "spells" after the first one, and she could, if left alone, sit and stare at one spot, in the woods behind her house, or at the beach or up on the Parkway, for hours at a time, so deep into wherever she had gone that it often took more than words to bring her back.

But by the ninth grade, she seemed to have outgrown the ghosts, seldom visited the "zones," as Virginia called them only when talking with her husband.

She was an excellent student and a beautiful girl, blonde and angular with a wide mouth and thick, full lips. She tanned well, and her skin, as sleek as she was, had a softness to it that hinted of a deeper lushness. She was warm to the touch, as if she had found a way to store the summer sun within her.

Blanchard was energetic and athletic. And, though some suspected her of secret snobbery because they couldn't see how it could be otherwise, she possessed impeccable manners.

They sent her to St. Catherine's her last two years of high school, at the same time James moved his family to Richmond. She seemed to do even better there; she was in her element among the city girls and the ones from other parts of the South whose parents sent them to Virginia to breathe the air of Lee and Jackson.

She did have to leave Sweet Briar once, her freshman year, after an unfortunate incident involving a boy from Washington and Lee, but the zones didn't really start reappearing until after she moved to New York.

James and Virginia were sure that Blanchard's "spells" were exacerbated by Manhattan psychiatrists who sent them bills on a regular basis. But Blanchard had been certain, after she was graduated with a degree in English, that she was going to New York. She caught on at a publishing house, working at a salary that, for the first two years, required that her parents subsidize her.

But Blanchard refused to live anywhere else for long. She went through two marriages, to a basketball coach at Long Island University and then to an English professor at NYU. Both marriages took her to the suburbs, first to Long Island and then to New Jersey. Both divorces took her right back to Manhattan.

The truth she never shared with anyone was that her principal horror was becoming the Tragic Southern Belle, something out of Tennessee Williams. She had seen women like that, growing up, women whose genes, rarefied upbringing and inclination to look back instead of forward had combined to make them hiders behind closed blinds, writers of irate letters to the newspaper editor, heeding voices that others never heard. It scared her how much she was like them, how easy it would be to become them.

She knew she sometimes did not act in a sane and responsible manner, but she and her analyst were working on it. She was certain, for a long time, that she was better off in New York, where somehow her eccentricities, her middle-of-the-night appearances in friends' lobbies, her diatribes against imagined demons, her zones, seemed more exotic, less pathetic, than they might have in a place like Richmond, where she would only remind others of an aunt in Staunton or a cousin in Southside.

The second marriage failed the day Blanchard came home early from her job as an editor at Random House and found a naked NYU coed in her bed. The girl smiled dreamily at her, stoned, while her husband's happy voice boomed out from the shower; he was singing a Beatles tune they'd once sung together, spontaneously, on a southbound train. The other passengers had clapped when they finished.

Blanchard was 44 the day she found the girl in her bed. She had really cared for the professor, with whom she had lived for 10 years. She had gone from full-time to part-time editing to please him. She was satisfied not to have children, because she knew he didn't want any. He was younger than she yet looked older, and he had added four sizes to his waist in their decade together, but she credited him with saving her after her first marriage fell apart.

But the naked coed, and the subsequent zone into which Blanchard fell, undid her. It resulted in the girl running down three flights of stairs, wearing only a bed sheet and seeking refuge behind the guard's desk from a middle-aged woman wielding a rather large butcher knife.

Blanchard was "hospitalized" for several days, and when she returned to the apartment, her husband, all his belongings and some of hers were gone. They only talked by telephone after that, and nothing came of it. Blanchard, given time and sanity enough to think, faced the truth: No matter what her husband said, it was close to impossible that she had come home early, for the first time in months, on the single day he had chosen to seduce one of his students.

She didn't have to be taken home to Richmond until almost a year later.

She had been erratic, off her medication and drinking heavily, yet she somehow kept her job and was even allowed to work full-time again as an editor. Some of her friends tried to help her and some disappeared. She told the ones who tried to help that she was fine, that she would snap out of it any day.

But then, in 1985, she was arrested for walking down Amsterdam Avenue at three in the afternoon, naked and singing a Beatles tune. She explained to the policeman who tried to cover her that she was too hot. It was mid-November.

And so, just in time for Thanksgiving, Blanchard Penn, who had re-assumed her family name after the first divorce and had never given it up again, was brought back south, accepting at last her fate. She lived with James and Virginia, who were already 72 and 66 and less thrilled to have their only daughter come home than they might have been 20 years before.

She told Betsy Traywick, one of the few old classmates who had stayed in touch since St. Catherine's days, that she needed to come home and take care of her mother and father. Everyone knew, though, that the care was essentially a three-way affair: The one most capable on any given day looked after the other two.

ELEVEN

DAVID LEAVES BLANCHARD and his father in the garden. He wants to call Carly and tell her that the car is not yet fixed, and see if anyone has called about a job interview. He would not be averse to a little sympathy.

He's irritated that she's not in her office at the moment. His concern is greatly aggravated because the secretary, a young woman not long out of a two-year community college with an associate degree in secretarial science, explains, "To tell you the truth, she's out showing a house right now."

Carly has told David that she does not completely trust Crystal.

"The thing is," she said to him one night at supper a few months ago, "I know in a heartbeat when she's lying. You know how some people say, 'Honestly' or 'Really' before they're going to tell one? With Crystal, it's 'To tell you the truth.' If Crystal starts a sentence with 'To tell you the truth,' watch your hat and coat."

It was good for a laugh, when David and Carly were still laughing together about things like that.

"I'll call back later," he tells Crystal, trying not to sound as peevish or desperate as he feels. "She can call here but, to tell you the truth, I'm going to be in and out."

David wonders what will become of him. He wonders what will become of them, of course, Carly and Frannie and Abbie. But he also believes, when he wakes up at four a.m. and can't get back to sleep, that they will be OK. About him, he's not so sure.

David wonders if he has taken a wrong turn somewhere. Other men, when they lose their jobs, seem able to recover.

They sell, or they simply charm, or they have some specialty that is invaluable to someone, somewhere.

What David has become an expert in, he knows when he mentally gathers his assets in the long, dark predawn, is a language. Not even a lot of languages. He can speak a little French, a little Italian. But mostly it's English. He is the guy who knows the difference between ground zero and square one. He can tell enormity from enormousness. He sneers at those who mistake masterful for masterly or write of meteoric rises.

He knows that kudos is singular. He held forth on that at a party one night when he'd had too much to drink and an acquaintance, a big, gregarious pharmaceutical salesman who made twice the salary David did when David had a job, misused it.

"Whoa," the man had said, his face reddening. "Who the fuck are you? The King of Kudos?" And David was the fool for correcting his friend.

That's me, David thinks to himself. The King of Kudos, indulged but hardly invaluable, kept for as long as the company stock doesn't dip.

He envies his father, who was born with the special talent that all small boys pray for — physical excellence. He knows that the Rail has suffered from having talents that he outlived before he was much past 35, and David is sure — usually sure — that another newspaper will pay him (sometime soon, please God) to report on some aspect of the human condition.

But he has seen the adoration on the faces of the other boys and the admiration of their fathers, and he knows that, were you to make him nine years old again, he would choose the quick reflexes and low, smooth, unflappable heartbeat of the Virginia Rail every time, and let the future be damned.

He knows that Neil Beauchamp didn't get to be who he was on natural talent alone. He knows that the soft suburban comfort his father afforded them when David was young helped ensure that he would not be a great athlete, the thing Neil would most have liked.

You should have been harder on me, David wants to tell his father. You shouldn't have just dropped in and out like some celebrity guest on a TV show.

He has seen The Contract, one of Neil Beauchamp's most treasured possessions, probably long since sold at some collectibles show, possessed by a father of three in Des Moines or a fat guy living in a trailer in Mobile.

He has heard his father, the only time Neil held forth at any length on the subject in his presence, talk about what The Contract meant, what it took him from, what it made him.

It was for $250, the amount to be given by the Detroit Tigers to James O'Neil Beauchamp, on January 8, 1953.

"This is what got me out of Penns Castle," he told David, who was 14 that year. They were living in a suburb of Kansas City while The Rail played out the string. "This is why we're here. Baseball." Even then, he said it as an evangelist might have said "Jesus."

Neil Beauchamp was a natural-born athlete. Everyone in town knew that.

They all assumed he would have been a better student, if he hadn't spent all his time working and playing ball.

Some of the older men, watching and drinking in the shade trees, thought he might even be a big-leaguer some day.

The more sober-minded, though, remembered Mack Turpin, who had thrown the ball so hard that they sometimes had to give the other team four strikes. Mack Turpin was working at the lumber yard, had been for a decade, after only a year in the low minors. They recalled Poorboy Ransom, who hit home runs so deep right before the war that the Jacksons put up a screen in their back yard, 75 feet beyond the railroad tracks. He joined the Marines in '42 and then went to work for Philip Morris in Richmond; he never even got an offer.

Big fish, they said. Little pond.

Neil's junior year, the Penns Castle Pirates beat every team they played. Twice they took on the city boys from John Marshall High, both times traveling to Richmond in the Blue Goose, a bus so beyond usefulness that it was deemed unsafe for everyday use on the regular school routes.

Twice, they won.

Neil hit two home runs in the first game, an 8-2 rout. The second time they played, they drew almost five thousand fans on a Wednesday afternoon. Most had come to see the Mosby Marvel, as Chauncey Durden, the *Times-Dispatch* sports editor, referred to him in his column.

In that one, they intentionally walked Neil the first four times he batted, and Penns Castle had only one unearned run through seven regulation innings, same as the city boys. Neil, playing center field, saved the game with a running catch in the bottom of the seventh with two runners on base and two out. He pitched in relief in the eighth and ninth, shutting out the home team.

Then, with Neil leading off the top of the tenth, the third pitcher, too proud to intentionally walk him again, trying to nibble him to death instead, threw a pitch that was too close to the plate. Neil drilled the ball over the shortstop's head, all the way to the fence, for a double.

The next batter popped up. Then, with an oh-two count on the skinny Pirates second baseman, Neil went for third. The batter swung and missed for strike three, but the catcher's throw was too late.

With two outs and Penns Castle's seventh batter at the plate, crouched down and waggling his bat as if his highest ambition was a walk, Neil waited through a ball and a strike.

Then, with the left-handed pitcher set to throw, his shadow almost reaching the third-base line in the dying light, Neil took off, his cleats throwing chunks of clay and small clouds of chalk. He caught the pitcher and catcher as well as his own coach unawares (although the man refused to admit later that he didn't give the signal to steal home).

The element of surprise would not have been enough, in itself. The pitcher recovered almost instantly and threw accurately to home, and the catcher jumped out of his crouch, pushing the batter aside.

Half a second before it happened, Neil Beauchamp was dead in the water. Everyone who saw it agreed to that. He had taken off his cap for his dash home and was holding it in his left hand. Not four feet from the plate, he stopped, and even in that he was, they all said, a natural. From full tilt to dead still, just like that.

The catcher seemed puzzled for a half-second. That was all it took. Suddenly, Neil was flat on his back, the heel of his left foot just scraping the plate, inches below the catcher's frantic swipe.

The John Marshall catcher swore he'd tagged him, and his coach was thrown out of the game taking up the cause, but the home-plate umpire had seen it all.

The bottom of the tenth was an anticlimax. The Richmond fans were so busy buzzing about the country boy who stole the game that they never really rallied behind their batters, who seemed equally distracted and went down in order, the last one rolling an easy grounder to the pitcher's mound that Neil pounced on and threw to first.

The Richmond fans didn't boo, although few could swear that Neil Beauchamp was either safe or out at the plate. They didn't cheer either, at the sight of their team losing for the second time to a country school that had fewer students than were in the John Marshall senior class. What they did, the sports editor noted the next day, was stand there watching silently, as if they realized this was something they would want to remember.

One of those who stood and watched was Jimmy Black. Jimmy was a short, quick man from Norfolk who scouted much of the eastern half of Virginia for the Detroit Tigers. He was as impressed as the rest, maybe more so, because he had seen Mickey Mantle run when he was in the minors, and he had seen Ted Williams swing a bat before he turned 19. He had seen Babe Ruth in his prime. His gift as a baseball talent scout was his ability to remember. And what Jimmy Black saw that day held up well against what he knew of potential greatness.

Jimmy Black was no fool, though. He didn't run out on the field and tell the kid he was the greatest prospect he'd ever discovered. That could be expensive, and one of Jimmy's most endearing qualities, from the Tigers' point of view, was the way he protected their money as if it were his. He'd been a scout for 30 years at least partly because of his thrift.

Besides, there was no reason to rush. Jimmy knew, because he knew all the other scouts who roamed his territory, that he alone had witnessed this.

There were plenty of high school studs who hit legendary home runs and ran like deer and struck out 18 batters in a game. The numbers didn't matter to Jimmy Black. Numbers were what the other guys let you do.

What mattered was how well they fit the mold, the interior vision that let some scouts, if they were lucky and experienced and perceptive enough, recognize greatness where it was not expected, be the first to truly identify it.

"I don't give a shit what their batting average is," he would say. "I don't care how many home runs they hit, how many men they struck out. All I care about's hit, hit with power, throw, run, field."

And in that one game, Jimmy Black, who was then 63 years old, thought he saw it all concentrated in one tall, thin country boy. He watched as Neil joined his teammates afterward in pushing an old, blue school bus until it reached sufficient speed for the coach to pop the clutch and start it.

He didn't talk to the boy, didn't let the sports editor or anyone else know he was there. It was the next-to-last game of the season, and the last one would be played in Penns Castle. If no other scout had seen Neil Beauchamp in Richmond, he could rest easy that none would come to Penns Castle.

Jimmy Black watched the last Penns Castle game, too, just to confirm what he already knew. And then he waited.

Neil didn't play summer ball, except on Saturdays with the town team when Wade Ramsey and his mother or some clerk were able to mind the store. Jimmy Black dropped by once, staying for half a game, just checking.

His senior year, Neil Beauchamp was a star on the football team, an end and a safety. Basketball was only six games old, and Christmas was just past, when Jimmy Black made his one visit to the Beauchamps' house.

He introduced himself to Jenny as a baseball scout. Jenny, who wondered what sort of grown man would have such a job title, directed Millie to run get her brother from the store.

"If I'd of known what he was coming for," she said later, her eyes red, "I would've run him off."

He wanted to make the offer before Neil's senior season began. Some of Jimmy Black's peers were rumored to be able to read, and he feared that they might be inspired enough to see this kid themselves if the newspaper persisted in writing about him.

They sat at the kitchen table, the older man drinking black coffee and Neil sipping a soda. What Jimmy Black was prepared to do, he said, was make it possible for Neil Beauchamp to be a professional ballplayer. He didn't oversell it, because he knew he could get most of these country boys for bus money. Hell, what else was there? The Army? The cigarette factory?

What the scout wanted to do was get Neil to sign on the spot and keep it a secret until the high school season was over.

"Then, we'll send you to Rookie League, soon as you graduate, and you're on your way."

Neil asked him if he had to wait until then.

Jimmy Black said no, he supposed not. He was only offering $250, and he wanted to be as accommodating as he could be without adding to that figure.

"Then," Neil said, "let's do it now."

Neil Beauchamp was not yet 18 years old, but he was tired. He was tired to death of working in the store, of going to school half-asleep and sitting in classes he wouldn't have found stimulating had he slept for 12 hours. He was not at all sure he was going to graduate.

He knew that his mother could use his help for as long as he was willing to give it, but he also knew she had a partner now, and he knew that, with all three of his half-siblings in school, she was as capable of staying afloat as she was ever going to be.

And, as he explained to Jenny later, this was the one chance he had to do something where he could make some real money, money he could send back home.

"If I'm not any good," he told her, "they'll send me back home quick enough, and you'll have more of me than you can stand."

He played another month and a half of basketball, and then he quit school and Penns Castle. The last thing he did, before he caught a ride into Richmond with Wade Ramsey to meet the Atlantic Coast Line train to Florida, was give Jenny half his signing bonus.

He had not wanted his family to come with him to Richmond, preferring to say his goodbyes at the only home of which he had much memory, all of them free to shed tears beyond the scrutiny of strangers.

He loved Jenny. They had been more of a team than mother and son, surviving William Beauchamp and then surviving without him. These days, Neil sees TV shows and hears stories about children who hold grudges their whole lives against parents who were too strict or too lenient or in some other way imperfect. He has never considered himself to be terribly forgiving, and he thinks at times that baseball permitted him to grow into one of the most immature creatures God ever made. But he does not feel he is capable of resenting Jenny O'Neil Beauchamp.

In 1982, a year when Neil Beauchamp's whole world seemed to be coming unraveled, Jenny would die suddenly of a massive heart attack, a year after she was able to let go of the store for good, turning its operation over to Tom. Neil would stand by her grave and wonder if the shock of not having to work day and night hadn't killed her.

Over the years, he has heard Millie, Willa and Tom all criticize aspects of their upbringing at one time or another, and he supposes that he is more tolerant because he grew up — once he discovered his talent — believing he was blessed. It made the work easier.

Neil Beauchamp was not surprised to find Jimmy Black sitting in his mother's kitchen that December night.

He knew he would be found.

On the way out of town that last day, with the smell of snow in the air and Florida already on his mind, a seemingly limitless life of baseball in front of him, Neil looked out the car window as they passed Penn's Castle.

He and James Penn hadn't spoken in years, their past going quickly from history to dim myth. After William Beauchamp left, Neil would sometimes be startled to realize that the man walking hurriedly past the front of the store, the man driving by in the Cadillac with his wife at his side, both of them looking straight ahead, had once been his father. Neil has never felt that his ability to forgive was more developed than anyone else's. What Neil has been able to do, to his gain and loss, is forget.

By the time he left, Neil's only real link to his first home was Blanchard. She went to all the ballgames that were played at Penns Castle, and he could often hear her voice, not louder than the others but of a different pitch. One of Neil's strengths was his ability, even then, to tune out what was not essential, at least on a ballfield. But he always heard Blanchard.

She would visit him at the store, learning which nights he worked and which of those were least likely to be busy. She remembered his birthday and sent him a gift at Christmas, obliging him to do the same for her, even though he couldn't afford it. Neil spent much of his time dealing with the very real needs of younger children, but by the time Blanchard was 12, he felt — though he never would have said this — that she was more or less his equal, even if she was five years younger.

He was sure she could have done a better job than he on some of his junior- and senior-year exams, even if she was thought by townspeople to be "peculiar."

But Neil enjoyed seeing the little blonde girl come into the store, usually starting her conversations with "Guess what?" and then launching into a breathless account of something that she made interesting by sheer dint of her enthusiasm. Blanchard would talk about her sixth-grade teacher, perfectly mimicking his slight stutter and mannerisms. She would savage the boys two years older than she who already were seeking her out in the hallways and at school dances and basketball games, finding humor in an overused phrase no one else had noticed, or a fashion failing only she had seen.

When word got out about the baseball contract, much of the town began holding a mostly unspoken grudge because Neil Beauchamp's departure meant an end to the glory by association he had brought them. No more would they be the Little Town with the Big Team.

When Blanchard came into the store on the first Tuesday night of 1953, she walked directly to the counter, where Neil was leaning, waiting for a Baptist deacon to decide whether he needed a dozen eggs or only half a dozen. She reached across, pulled his head down toward hers, and kissed him right on the lips.

Neil had only been kissed on the lips by a couple of girls his own age. He blushed; Blanchard didn't.

"I just want you to know," she told him, her voice low and conspiratorial, "that I am very, very proud of you."

It sounded so adult. He might have laughed if he hadn't looked into her eyes.

That last day, when Neil glanced out the window of Wade Ramsey's Studebaker, he saw something small and red standing by the road. When they passed by, Ramsey slowed down, not knowing whether the figure before him in the icy mist was going to step into the road or hold still.

As they passed, not going 10 miles an hour, Blanchard dropped the hood from her head and waved.

Had she gone to fetch the mail or the paper? Neil was certain no one in Penns Castle, other than his mother and her other children, knew exactly when he was leaving.

But Blanchard was there, waiting.

When he looked back as Wade Ramsey speeded up, the figure in red had turned and was watching his departure as if she meant to blink only when there was no more of him to see at all.

TWELVE

BLANCHARD JUMPS WHEN she looks back and sees Neil standing there, staring at her.

When she recovers, she leans over to pick up the flowers she's cut. Without a word, she turns from him and starts walking, her basket over her right wrist. Neil follows her down the old brick walkway, away from the house. Grass and moss have made inroads in the mortar, but he sees that Blanchard has planted rosebushes along the sides, outlining the trail to the gazebo.

She had to pay a man with a bush hog to come in and clear the space around the old structure, so that now you can see eastward for several miles, as you could when Blanchard was a girl.

She and Neil sit inside the renovated latticework and look out toward Richmond. A red-tailed hawk sails before them in the November current, waiting for food to reveal itself in the valley below.

"Do you remember?" Blanchard asks him, ignoring his silent prayer for forgetfulness, or at least quiet.

"Yes," he says, after a time.

She puts her left hand over his right one, and neither of them speaks.

Until that Florida spring of 1953, Neil Beauchamp had never been outside Virginia. He was a high school dropout with no money or social skills.

What saved him, he supposed later, was a lack of need, an immunization from distraction.

Neil Beauchamp was there to play baseball. He did not pine away for letters from home. He did not shrink from the abuse and coarse jokes of older players (and they were all older, except a couple of 16-year-olds from Puerto Rico who spoke almost no English), did not desire a softer bed or better buses, did not need more spending money.

Neil believes that he would have agreed, in the spring of 1953, to camp out every night on the lush Southern outfield grass, never stepping outside the fences, with unknown flowers scenting the air, if those had been the conditions for him to play baseball.

He wandered around town when he had a rare few hours off. Often he went alone, pleased beyond words to be in a place where people picked oranges and grapefruit off trees, where there was no store to help run, no brood of children to herd from danger like a border collie, where there was no other work than the playing of baseball. He felt guilty for his mother's sake, and he sent her more money than he kept.

"I know times are hard right now," he wrote Jenny two weeks after he left, in response to a gloomy letter, "but I am hopeful that, sometime soon, I can make things easier for us all." He was trying to appease his mother, but he really believed he was better than most of the ragged prospects with whom he shared dugouts and meals.

When he found a minor-league hitting instructor who was willing to spend time with him, he almost wrecked the man's health, begging him to pitch batting practice to him, to tell him all he knew.

"Son," the hitting instructor said after a few days, "I'm afraid to mess with your swing anymore. You swing pretty damn good right now."

He said it partly to get Neil off his back, but he knew, like Jimmy Black, that this boy was special.

Jimmy Black himself showed up at the Tigers' training camp in early March. He came by "to make sure they're treating you right," offering to go see Jenny and assure her that "her boy" was thriving, hinting that he hoped Neil would not forget him when he hit the big time.

Neil competed against an assortment of players in spring training, some who had actually been in the majors. They would play once or twice a day, and one day early on, a coach walked up to him and told him he was a third baseman. The logic behind this was never explained to him, but he seemed to play as well there as he had been playing in the outfield. He was willing to take extra fielding practice, and anything he did not field cleanly, he stopped with his body, positioning himself so the ball would bounce forward, where he could pounce on it and use his strong arm and quick release to throw out the runner.

His hitting, though, was what made people look up from what they were doing. He had such a whip of a stroke, clean and smooth, without a hitch. His bat always seemed to be in the same plane as the approaching ball, meeting it level and effortlessly, returning it in such a manner that, very often, the only way to get him out was to manage to have a fielder stationed within a foot or two of the place where Neil Beauchamp's line drives screamed past. His bat was a scythe cutting the humid air. It was worth watching him miss, one coach said, just to see the whole, unimpeded swing.

His hitting was what got him into trouble with Buddy Wainwright.

On the third of March, Neil was batting for the Single-A team, filling in for a 22-year-old who had the flu. Batting third, he led off the sixth inning. He swung on the first pitch and hit the ball so perfectly that veterans two fields away stopped and turned, drawn by a sound they couldn't define but knew on the rare instances when they heard it.

"You know," Jimmy Black told Neil later, "you might swing at a million balls, and you might hit two or three on the exact, dead-solid sweet spot, the one that's so clean that it don't even make a lot of noise. Just wood and ball, like there was nothing else in the world."

Neil had hit a few like that before, but he didn't say anything to the man who had signed him. They were talking on the night after his perfect hit, and he was shining Buddy Wainwright's shoes.

The ball had never gotten more than 40 feet off the ground. When it cleared the fence in left-center, it might have been only half that high. It yielded to gravity very grudgingly, and when it reached Buddy Wainwright's car, a hundred feet past the fence, it was at the perfect elevation.

It smashed the windshield with such authority that a gleeful "uh-oh" emanated from snowbirds and local fans throughout the complex, all sure it was someone else's plate glass. Children and adults rushed from the various fields to find the home-run ball and see the damage.

And Neil, rounding the bases, trying not to show the tingle of pride he felt, heard someone shout, "Kid's in for it now. That's Buddy's car."

Wainwright had led the American League in home runs twice, once before the war and once afterward, and he was near the end of a long and mostly distinguished career. His maroon convertible Buick was his pride and joy; Neil had seen him driving around Lakeland in it, usually with one or two young women sharing the front seat.

The Buick's windshield was so thoroughly smashed by Neil Beauchamp's perfect home run that shards were found inside the next car over.

After the game, Neil looked up to see Buddy Wainwright standing by the fence next to the dugout. His large, round face, its festive centerpiece a bulb of a nose with a crease down the middle, seemed redder than usual.

"C'm'ere" he said, and Neil noticed then that two of the other Tiger veterans were with him.

Neil approached him hesitantly.

"Yes, sir. I'm sorry about your car."

"Sorry?" Wainwright looked at his two teammates, who seemed to be enjoying themselves. "Sorry? Look, country boy, I park my goddamn car a block from the ballpark, I don't expect to have it ruined. Now, what are you goin' to do about it?"

Neil did not know what he could do about it, and said so.

Wainwright had been slouching against the wire fence. He eased himself up.

"Well, I tell you what. You got some payin' back to do. You can either pay me for that windshield or work it out."

Neil said he supposed he would have to work it out.

"Be at my room at six tonight," Wainwright said. "Don't be late." And the three veteran players turned and left.

That evening at 5:45, Neil knocked on Buddy Wainwright's door. Unlike the minor leaguers, whose living conditions could border on the primitive, Wainwright and the other players who, it was assumed, would make the major-league roster, lived in relative luxury. The motel where Buddy Wainwright resided had a pool. It had an actual lobby.

After the third knock, Wainwright came to the door, looking as if he had been awakened from a sound sleep.

"What!" he said, then recognized the boy who had wrecked his car.

He went away from the door without a word and came back holding his spikes and a stained baseball uniform.

"I want you to shine these shoes, and I want you to get this cleaned," he said. "The damn equipment man does a piss-poor job of cleaning. I want you to find somewhere where they can clean my damn uniform so it's white."

Neil took the bundle without a word.

"Have it to me by tomorrow morning," Wainwright yelled after him. "Don't be late. Leave it outside."

For three weeks, Neil did Buddy Wainwright's bidding. Shoes to shine, errands to run, gloves to re-web, bats to tape. On one occasion, Wainwright even foisted a less-than-desirable date off on the player he had taken to calling "Virginia." Neil rode with the woman, who was three years older than he and had a car, to a liquor store. He choked down his first beer sitting in a drive-in parking lot, and afterward, he kissed her goodnight. Her breath smelled of tobacco and bad teeth, and when she suggested they go dancing, he told her he had to be back by 11, because of curfew.

"Buddy don't have to be back by eleven," she said.

"That's because he's a star," Neil said, and left her sitting there.

The first time Neil Beauchamp stepped on a golf course was as Buddy Wainwright's caddy, and Wainwright had a wonderful time demanding an assortment of 10-irons, short niblicks and other phantom clubs while the other veterans with whom he was playing grinned.

Neil was well into the month when someone told him that the car's windshield was insured, that it didn't cost Buddy Wainwright a dime, but he already understood the rules by then. Neil had seen what happened to younger players who resisted the harassment thrown their way by bored veterans. They were said to have bad attitudes, and it seemed to Neil that unfortunate things happened to these more easily offended players. And he saw that the veterans didn't even bother making life a living hell for the ones who didn't stand out, the ones who had no chance of making it.

Buddy Wainwright's bullying, Neil came to see, was another indication of what he already knew. He, by God, was going to make it.

The day the veterans headed north, Buddy Wainwright came by the cottage Neil shared with a homesick shortstop from Waycross, Georgia.

Wainwright had a bat in his hand and a fierce enough expression on his face that Neil did not step from the shadows of the room at first.

"Here, Virginia," the veteran told him. "I hit six home runs this spring with this sucker. You damn sure better take care of it. And you better not hit my fuckin' car with it."

Neil took the bat, saying thank you to Buddy Wainwright's back. He did not find out until the maroon Buick convertible was somewhere beyond the Lakeland city limits that the Tigers had decided they could not afford to keep an aging slugger who either homered or struck out, much more of the latter than the former, and who was too fat to bend all the way down for ground balls at first base.

The story about Buddy Wainwright and his gullible minor-league caddy made the rounds, and Neil came to understand that he had bettered his stock by playing his assigned role.

He could, it was agreed in rooms where futures were decided, take it. So many of them couldn't, the cigar-smokers said, shaking their heads. Not like it was before the war. You had to take it then.

Neil Beauchamp would, of course, have been only a happy hod carrier without the sweet swing. But he batted over .400 that spring against other young men who would soon be assigned to play in places like Kinston and Jamestown and Lubbock. He was capable, as they all knew, of memorable home runs, but Neil's strength, then and later, would be his ability to hit hard, straight, predictable, unstoppable line drives, to not be seduced by the fences.

They sorted out the minor-league players two weeks before they broke camp. Neil would play on a Class D team in

Valdosta, Georgia, a short trip north. He hitched a ride with an older player, and the only things he took that he hadn't brought south in February were his home and road uniforms and Buddy Wainwright's black bat.

He batted .360 in Valdosta, best in the league. He used the black bat only a dozen times all year, never making a big deal of it, never admitting the possibility that such a thing as luck existed, never telling anyone that he had four singles, two doubles and two home runs with Buddy's bat. One of the home runs was a grand slam that encouraged the country people in attendance to pass the hat and present him with forty-seven dollars and thirty-eight cents at the end of the game.

Once that summer, Jenny and the children took the train down, staying in a boarding house for two nights, so they could watch Neil wear out half of the Tallahassee pitching staff.

That fall, he went back to Penns Castle and worked at the store, trying to make up for all the time he was gone. Whenever the weather allowed, he'd get high school kids, some of them former teammates, to pitch to him at the old field behind the gym, the younger boys chasing the balls down in the outfield. In an interview years later, he said that he became even more of a line-drive hitter in that way, because if he had developed a long-ball swing, he would have lost all the baseballs to the woods behind the right-field fence.

Neil Beauchamp had teammates, in his three minor-league seasons, who seemed to waste whole careers in one winter. They would hit over .300 or win 18 games, then swagger off in September. Then, next spring, they'd arrive in Florida 20 pounds heavier, somehow distracted from the one thing most of them could do well. And then they would be gone.

Neil thought that perhaps the difference was that they had not staked their entire lives on baseball. He could not understand them, but he could learn from them. He never let up.

Neil hit .344 at Durham and Little Rock in 1954, tearing up the Carolina and Southern leagues. That winter, he was invited to play on one of the Cuban winter league teams and sent money home to his mother from Cienfuegos.

"Seems like I've found a way," he wrote in one postcard, "to miss winter entirely." He estimated that, between spring training, the minor-league season and the winter league, he had played in almost 250 baseball games in 1954. He does not remember a happier time.

The next year, he batted .364 with 13 home runs and 105 runs batted in at Charleston, West Virginia, in the International League, sending home postcards from Havana and Montreal, which Jenny would paste to the back of the store's cash register.

He spent September of 1955 on the bench in Detroit, where many of the veterans knew him already from spring training. The Detroit sports writers knew him, too, had been following him for three seasons in The Sporting News box scores, were proud they'd seen him hit one "at least six hundred feet" in Florida. They tipped off the fans, and when Neil Beauchamp first stepped up to the plate at Briggs Stadium, people nudged their less-savvy neighbors and pointed to the game program. "That's him," they'd say. "That's the one I told you about."

And he never looked back, never spent another day in the minor leagues. He hit .293 his rookie year, with 12 home runs. The next time he hit under .300, he would be well into his 30s.

"He is as thin as a rail," the sports columnist at one of the Detroit papers wrote in May of 1956, "and his swing is as flat and level as one, not a wiggle or a hitch, so pure and solid you could drive a locomotive over it." The headline the copy desk put on the column would stick to Neil for the rest of his life: "The Virginia Rail." The sports columnist's obituary would

list among his accomplishments giving Hall-of-Famer Neil
Beauchamp his nickname.

Blanchard leads Neil on a path she has worn down, along
the crest of the ridge. They walk through tulip poplars and
oaks, past a couple of mounds signifying the openings to long-
abandoned dropshaft mines, where many decades of branches,
leaves and dirt cover holes more than 100 feet deep.

The trail fades away, and Neil has to trust Blanchard's
sense of direction. Louder and louder, he can hear the short
bursts, the mechanical grunts, of earth-moving equipment, of
Caterpillars and backhoes. Soon, Neil sees red earth through
the almost-bare trees.

Blanchard stops just short of the clearing, where they are
still hidden from the workers below.

"Can you believe this shit?"

The construction crews are making the most of the last
good weather, trying to complete the DrugWorld building
before the first snow. The cinder-block walls are being
covered with brick that is only slightly redder than the
wounded clay on which they stand. Several roofers are beginning their work on the steep Dutch colonial pitch. The
hammering has a rhythm that will carry the men to suppertime.

"When they first started," she says, "after it was clear that
Jimmy Sutpen and the rest of those thieves at the courthouse
weren't going to do a damn thing, I'd sneak down here. . . ."

Blanchard is suddenly seized by a fit of giggling. It takes
her a long two minutes to regain control.

"I would sneak down here," she finally continues, "and I'd
put sugar in their gas tanks. I did it three times, and then I got
scared to do it any more.

"I got pretty good at it, really. I think I might have a flair
for guerrilla warfare. I'd reach the spot where that thick clay

started, and I'd put on a pair of Daddy's old shoes that I'd brought along. So they would think it was some man. Then I'd take the shoes off when I got back to that spot and walk back to the house. I'd wash Daddy's old shoes and hide 'em in one of the old plunder rooms.

"But it really messed up their party, I'll tell you that. They'd lose a day or two like that."

Blanchard lets out a long sigh.

"Of course, it was like spitting in the wind. Pretty soon, they'd be right back at it again. And then they started posting guards every night."

She gives Neil a look and a wink.

"They took the guards off last week, though. I guess they thought whoever it was had given up. FFC."

Neil looks at her.

"Fat fucking chance," she says, and turns again to watch the workers.

"You ought to be careful," Neil suggests, but she doesn't seem to hear him.

They walk back the way they came, soon finding the path. Their shoes are caked with red mud, and Blanchard says she'll clean them as soon as they get back to the house.

They are almost to the gazebo again when the deer crashes out of the woods. It bounds over the ridge and is out of sight down the hill before they can walk over to watch.

THIRTEEN

DAVID WANDERS THROUGH the house. He has called the garage this time and is assured that his wounded car is getting top priority.

There is a photo wall in an alcove at the back of the great room. He is surprised to see how many of the pictures framed and hanging there are of Neil Beauchamp. Some are from newspaper clippings, some are promotional glossies, apparently designed to make the players look as foolish as possible. There is one taken at the kind of function the Tigers and later the Indians would have every year. In it, Neil Beauchamp, Number 7, is squatting beside his young son, who is dressed in an identical Detroit uniform. David guesses that he would have been four, because the year after that, the Virginia Rail was traded.

David does not recall any photograph taken at a later date in which either he or his father looked so genuinely happy.

Neil Beauchamp figures he would have made another $5 million playing baseball had he been born five years later, still ripe when the free-agent money started pouring in during the mid-'70s. By the early '90s, he could make more signing his old baseball cards and children's bats and gloves than he did as a player in his prime.

When he was still making such appearances, Neil and old acquaintances would laugh and shake their heads about the strangeness of it all. Some of them were bitter, railing about the millionaire .240 hitters, the porcelain outfielders who were good for only 100 games a year, the rag-arm pitchers with losing records who made more than whole teams did 20 years before.

Neil, though, would trade none of it for what he had. He can't imagine how wealth could have made any of it better. His sole regret, large enough to blot out all the others' bitter, small complaints, is that it ended.

He thought $20,000 and 154 games a year were all he ever ought to ask for.

When he was introduced to Catherine Anne Taylor, that magic rookie year when he had steaks for breakfast and rode in plush and important trains smelling of grandeur and comfort that would never be matched by any jet, he was drawing a salary of $10,000 a year and sending some of that home.

What did he need with money? His meals were paid for, his hotel on the road was paid for, his train ticket, even his clothes, thanks to clothing stores that asked only that he drop around on the odd off afternoon to sign some baseballs and shake some hands. He still made extra money playing down south in the winter leagues.

And there were girls.

Neil turned 21 at his fourth Lakeland spring training; he hit two singles and a double that day.

He was not handsome. His teeth had not been fixed yet, and when he was forced to smile at something, his left hand went up involuntarily to cover the lower half of his angular face.

But he was tall and thin, and he had the power — not the power of politicians and tycoons, either, offering young women gilded luxury tempered by sweat-stained pillows and bodies best abided in dark chambers. Neil Beauchamp's power was that he drew the people, made the cameras flash, carried whomever he was with into the center of the excitement with him, while he was still as untouched by time as a Greek statue (albeit one with bad teeth). He was the New Boy.

He made love to two girls that spring. The first was a tall redhead five years his senior who, he later discovered, had been with two of his teammates already. The second, a blonde education major down from a Midwestern college, spent the better part of a week with him. He was not a voracious lover, neither devoured by want nor the need to prove himself, but he was sometimes dazzled that year by all the women, young and old, who sought him out. He only occasionally paused to think that, should he have met one of those women at a bar, dressed in his cheap slacks and short-sleeved striped shirt (he had six that all vaguely resembled each other), none of them would acknowledge his existence, much less remove her clothes and offer to do anything, anything you want, Neil.

But Neil Beauchamp was not really dazzled, relatively speaking. He did not spend half his first year's salary on a new Chrysler, like the fellow rookie, a pitcher, with whom he would room when they headed north. He did not have to hide from irate husbands or boyfriends or face paternity suits or assault charges, or worry very much about the clap. He was, it was agreed, quiet. The way he was hitting, he was allowed to be any way he wanted.

"Don't you get him laid," one of the coaches warned an older player who was known to share his bounty with promising youngsters. "If he ain't gettin' laid now, a lay sure as hell couldn't make him any better."

Maybe, Neil would think much later, he would have been better off if he had catted around, accepting all offers, working up some emotional calluses.

But Kate Taylor changed that, and he did not, at that point in their courtship, resist the change.

She was working that summer, between her junior and senior years at Michigan, in the Tigers' front office. She was thin, with a long face and a jaw that was just strong enough. She had raven hair, a perfect nose and a look — at once the dreaminess of small children and the promise of abandon — that was defined by the Tigers' veterans, some of whom had tried to take her out for drinks, as "bedroom eyes."

She chose Neil Beauchamp, who would have been too shy, even in that year when he was discovered by most of the population of a major American city, to choose her.

He was embarrassed by his lack of education, painfully aware that his expertise was limited mostly to trains, hotels and baseball. He could not have pointed out the other cities in the American League on a blank map. He was essentially lost when he turned the daily newspaper away from the sports section or the comics. On the Tigers' second trip to New York that season, he had asked the traveling secretary what the distant structure was, towering over all the buildings around it.

"Jesus," the man said, shaking his head, "didn't you see *King Kong?*"

Neil would never have gone after a woman like Catherine Anne Taylor, so self-assured, possessing secret knowledge of matters cultural and carnal to which, he was sure, he would never be privy.

She had rejected several of his teammates, all more worldly than he, and he was stunned when she asked him one night, when he was walking out the players' exit after a loss to the Orioles, if he would give her a ride home.

Neil said he would, cursing himself for not combing his hair more carefully, for not dressing better before leaving his rooming house for the ballpark, for not keeping mouthwash in his locker.

They stopped twice so Neil could sign autographs for children. He almost forgot to open the used Chevy's door for her, taking her cue finally as she stood unmoving and patient beside the car.

Inside, her perfume, less sweet, more nuanced than the cheap, bold fragrances his occasional dates wore, made his knees weak.

They were almost out of the parking lot when she spoke.

"If you don't know where I live," she said quietly, smiling slightly, "how are you going to drive me home?"

"Maybe," he said, his voice scratchy from nerves, "maybe I don't want to drive you home."

"Well, where do you want to drive me, then?"

"Where do you want to be driven?"

She smiled again, looking straight ahead.

"You decide."

Neil stopped at the entrance to Michigan Avenue.

"I don't know anywhere to take a girl as pretty as you."

He had never been good at repartee. He envied the Northern boys, who spit out in machine-gun bursts the words that tumbled around in his slow mouth like marbles.

But this one time, he felt he had said the right thing.

She moved closer to him. He could feel her thigh against his.

"Turn here," she said. "I know a place."

Before the summer was over, they were an item. That winter, Neil went south again to Cuba for the last time. He wrote her every day, and she wrote him every day. His letters were about dusty bus rides and cockfights and ballparks where gamblers with guns gave the evil eye to errant batsmen. Hers were about philosophy classes and sorority parties and the annual trip to close down her parents' cottage on the eastern side of Lake Michigan.

In December, she flew down to Havana for a week, with her parents' permission, and she and Neil, who everyone assumed had been "doing it" for months, made love for the first time in a hotel room near the harbor. The drums and horns of Latin music from a wedding reception drifted into their open window from somewhere on the street below, defining the rhythm of their passion.

By February, they were engaged. Kate's parents allowed her to spend a week in Florida. It unnerved Neil to be around the Taylors, partly because they knew two things, as hard as they tried to hide this knowledge: They were above him, and he was screwing their daughter.

Neil would come to understand, in the good and bad years that followed, what he brought to the Taylors' table. He would come to appreciate Kate's keen eye for talent, her understanding in the summer of 1956 that the gangly, hungry country boy she saw taking extra batting practice every day was the genuine article, the player who would only get better, the one who would leave his mark.

Kate Taylor loved baseball, and she enjoyed being around men who made their living by their testosterone. She did not intend, as she told one of her sorority sisters one night when they were both drunk, to marry "some limp-dick fratty-bagger living off his daddy's money."

On the other hand, she did not intend to cast her lot with one of the oafs who occasionally and unsuccessfully sought her. She sensed who would drink and party his way out of the league too soon, which ones would never be strong enough to make it at all, which ones were bullies who would use their power to humiliate anyone — including their wives — they could control.

Her father, a man who started out as a used-car salesman and wound up owning two automobile dealerships, had told her all her life that she was in a position, because of who they were, to choose.

And Kate chose Neil Beauchamp.

Neil saw, too, that she brought more than her beauty and intelligence to their unlikely union. She was able to smooth his edges without his even realizing they were being smoothed. She took him places, introduced him to people who didn't really give a damn whether the Virginia Rail's subjects and verbs agreed or not, were just happy to have a .300 hitter at their party. She took him to museums, talked about books and movies, never educating, just telling him stories, mentioning things that "somebody told me once" without ever intimating that these were things any educated person should know.

They were married in June of 1957, and for a very long time, Neil Beauchamp thought his life was complete.

David was born in March of 1959, while Neil was in Lakeland. He flew home to see his new son and was back in Florida two days later.

He had driven in 121 runs the year before and batted almost .350. He was in the midst of a three-year run that would establish him as one of the best hitters in baseball. He was, with Kate's guidance, becoming a fixture in Detroit, the man people called to make an appearance at a fund-raiser, to ride a float in the Christmas parade. The Rail was quiet, they agreed, but he didn't drink too much, like some of them did, and he would keep his hands off the butts of their wives and daughters. He was polite enough, for a ballplayer.

He stayed north in the winter now, and while part of him missed playing almost every day, he loved Kate, and while there were times he needed to be by himself, he cherished the unaccustomed feeling of warmth that she brought to the coolness of his life.

When he went to spring training that year, he offered, over and over again, to stay with her in Detroit and let 'em fine him. They weren't going anywhere without the Virginia Rail.

"No," she'd told him. "You've got your job to do. Your job is to make me proud."

Standing by her bed, the day after David was born, Neil took Kate's hand in his. He kneeled and kissed it.

"Are you proud of me?" she had asked him, and he thought there was something sad in the way she asked it.

"I am always proud of you," he told her.

Kate just smiled and closed her eyes.

FOURTEEN

THE COPPER-HAIRED mechanic is a short, stout boy wearing a dark blue baseball cap with "Ford" across the front. He might not yet be out of high school, might not ever be out of high school, but here he seems to know that he holds all the cards.

"Well, I'll tell you," he says to David. "I got to be home by seven, and I got to pick up some stuff for my girl at the grocery store for Thanksgiving dinner. So, I expect you'd be alright coming back at six. I'm almost sure I'll have it fixed by then."

In the short time David has been in the garage, the car's chances of being repaired today have dipped from "definitely" to "almost sure."

"I'll be back about 5:45," he tells the boy, who only chews and nods.

David wonders if it is too late to rent a car for two days, wonders if any car rentals will be open when he comes back in two hours and finds either the car not fixed or the feckless mechanic already gone. He wonders why he hesitates, why he doesn't just call Hertz or Avis, charge whatever it costs. He could be home in time to tell Frannie and Abbie a bedtime story. He supposes he hates to admit he's wasted so much time already; he thinks of himself as a lottery regular who plays the same number every day and won't change for fear it will come in the first time he drops it.

Back at Blanchard's, he parks the truck and goes into the empty house. He can see her and his father at the far edge of the back yard, sitting in the gazebo. She seems, from this distance, to be leaning on Neil. They might be, from David's vantage point, teenagers on a date.

Blanchard has given them a desultory tour of the old place. The study particularly caught David's eye, full of books from four generations of Penns, books from Blanchard's New York days, more books than he has ever seen in a private home, stacked to the high ceiling in the built-in bookcases along all four walls, with boxes of them taking up half the available floor space.

It is to this dark, comfortable room, this womb scented by ancient paper, that David wanders now.

There is no order to it; some of the books were left when James and Virginia and their daughter moved to Richmond in 1954. Some were brought back by Blanchard when she reclaimed the old house.

A Twain collection's neighbors are Kafka and Belva Plain. A *National Geographic* collection running from the late '50s until the present takes up most of one shelf along one wall, and children's books from before World War II sit no more than half a dozen volumes from Henry Miller. *Bellefleur* and the works of Balzac are only coincidentally neighbors. Greek philosophy and *Reader's Digest* condensed books battle for the scant light a lone window provides.

The late afternoon sun spotlights the dust motes disturbed by David's invasion. He walks the length of one wall, remembering the guilty comfort of childhood libraries, when he should have been outside, trying to be a better baseball player.

There are scrapbooks here and there. David glances through some of them — mostly keepsakes from happier, brighter days at Penn's Castle. James and Virginia's wedding takes up one full album, as do Blanchard's elementary school years. There is no obvious evidence of James Penn's first marriage.

In the corner, though, is an album, sitting on the next-to-bottom shelf, that has a title pasted across its spine, in letters an inch high. The letters look as if they might have been drawn by a child, and the album, unlike most of the books in this room, seems to have been explored in the recent past. There are holes in the front and back covers, and on the shelf next to it is an opened lock.

Picking the album up, David can smell, even through the dust and old paper, Blanchard.

Inside are clippings highlighting the career of the Virginia Rail, from high school write-ups in the *Richmond Times-Dispatch* to features in the Detroit papers and *Sports Illustrated*. Interspersed are handwritten notes, like pages from a diary, the earliest one on cheap, lined school paper. "Neil waved at me today." "Neil looked so handsome today. He's gotten his hair cut short for summer." "Neil won't let them pick on me. All I have to do is say the word, and he'll protect me."

There are, here and there, poems.

The pages are, for the most part, dated. On one, with "February 14, 1955" across the top in confident, showy penmanship, is written, over and over as if done for an after-school blackboard punishment, "I love Neil Beauchamp. I love Neil Beauchamp. I love Neil Beauchamp." It fills the page, perhaps 200 repetitions of the same sentence.

"You do remember, though? You didn't forget?"

Neil is staring straight out into the valley to the east. Blanchard is pressed hard against his right side. He lifts his arm and she slides even closer.

Should Neil Beauchamp live forever, it would not be long enough to forget Valentine's Day, 1955.

He was still a minor-leaguer, still going to the islands every winter to play more baseball, still coming back home for a scant few weeks between seasons, his contributions to the store becoming more and more of a monetary nature. He was fairly certain they'd move him up to Triple-A when the season started, a step away from the big leagues. He was on track.

That morning, he helped Wade Ramsey open up, then stocked the shelves, applied a layer of paint to the old office, worked the counter for a while. Around one that afternoon, as he was getting ready to go for lunch at the Castle Grill three doors down, the phone rang, and he answered.

"Neil? Is that you? Neil, I'm in trouble. Can you come? Please?"

He still saw her from time to time, even though the Penns had moved out of their castle and into Richmond the year before. She wrote him during his summers in Georgia or Pennsylvania, during his winters in Cuba, and he would send back postcards. She always knew when he was coming home, and she'd arrange to see him. She couldn't drive yet, and they would often meet at the lunch counter at one of the downtown department stores. He was supposed to meet her at one of them in two days.

"What's wrong?"

He knew Blanchard was capable of over-dramatization. Once, the fall before, she had lured him to Richmond, where he picked her up on a street corner in the West End, two blocks from her house. "This is deadly urgent," she had told him, and the problem had turned out to be no more than a wandering boyfriend.

This was different, though.

"They want to put me in jail, Neil. Daddy is going to kill me."

The problem was a watch. It wasn't even much of a watch, it seemed to Neil, surely not worth the risk. The clerk in the Broad Street jewelry store had seen her slip it into her handbag and he and another clerk stopped her in the parking lot, heading for a bus back home. The girlfriend with whom she was skipping half a day of school ran away, leaving Blanchard to first deny that she had the watch and then beg them to let her make one phone call to a friend who would straighten things out.

"I'll be there in half an hour," he said, and then he had to talk on the phone with the store manager, urging him to not call the police just yet, that he would make everything right.

Neil was barely 20, and he had no idea how he might actually make things right. He stopped by the house, on his way into Richmond, thinking he would need his checkbook. In a corner of his room, he spied the old black bat, the one Buddy Wainwright had given him two years before. In a flash of inspiration, he grabbed the bat and threw it into the back seat of his car.

By the time he got to the store, in downtown Richmond, it was almost two o'clock.

Blanchard was in the manager's office. She apparently had been trying to convince a gray-haired man in a somber black suit that her friend had slipped the watch into her purse, but she didn't want to give the friend's name.

She ran to Neil and hugged him, crying.

"Don't let them take me away," she said. "Don't let them tell Daddy."

Neil had never been in a jewelry store before. In his wrinkled white shirt and work trousers, he would not have been mistaken for a serious customer.

The manager, though, knew him. Blanchard had told him that the man coming to her rescue was none other than Neil Beauchamp, who was going to be in the big leagues any time now, maybe this year. The manager read the sports pages, and he remembered the column that had been done on Neil the previous December. The headline had asked, "Penns Castle to Briggs Field?" It left no doubt as to the answer.

"You've got quite a talent, son," the man told him, after reciting some of the particulars of the column to Neil. "Be careful that you don't get messed up like some of 'em do when they hit it big." Neil imagined that part of the man's idea of "messed up" involved associating with female kleptomaniacs.

"Can we talk in private, sir?" Neil asked him, and the two of them walked outside, leaving Blanchard sitting in the manager's office.

"I've known her all my life," Neil told the man. "She's not a bad girl, just a little wild. Is there anything I can do that will keep her from getting this on her record? I'll be glad to pay for the watch, anything you want for it."

The manager, enthralled though he was to have a future big-leaguer in his presence, did not want to let matters drop. He did not think it was right to let somebody steal and get away with it.

"I think it would be good for her to have to deal with this, and not have somebody fix everything for her," the manager said before going silent. "I'm going to have to get the authorities in on this. Let her daddy take care of it, if he can. I know of the Penns, and I know he's a fine man. He'd like to make sure she didn't do anything like this again, I'll bet.

"Besides, everybody that works here knows what she did. How will it look if I let her go?"

"Well, you wouldn't have to let anybody know, would you?"

The man shook his head. He had decided, it appeared to Neil, that he was going to stand his ground on this, no matter what.

Neil thought about it, and then asked the manager to come over to the car with him.

The man shrugged and then followed him.

Neil opened the door and reached into the backseat. He pulled out the old black bat. The manager took a half step back in alarm, until he saw that Neil did not intend to pummel him with it.

"You remember Buddy Wainwright?" Neil asked.

The manager nodded. "Led the league in home runs two times."

Neil explained about Buddy Wainwright's bat, how Buddy had given it to him in 1953, the same day they cut him, how it had been Neil's good-luck charm, how he'd gone 8 for 12 with it, never using it except when he really needed it.

"If you'll let me pay you for that watch and let her go," he told the man, "I'll give you this bat."

"And, sir, not to be bragging, but one day I'll be in the major leagues, and that bat will be worth even more than it is now."

The man stood with his hands in his pockets for half a minute. Then he took the bat, holding it as if he were appraising its true value.

Finally, he just said, "Deal."

Neil wrote him a check on the hood of his car, then waited outside while the man went back to his office and showed Blanchard out the back door, telling her that she was lucky to have such a friend as Neil Beauchamp.

Neil thought the man might be so impressed with his offering that he would let Blanchard go and tell him to keep the bat. It was Neil's intention to emphasize how far he was willing to go to keep his half-sister out of trouble without actually having to pay the price. He loved the old black bat Buddy Wainwright gave him as much as it was possible to love an inanimate object.

But the man took the bat, and he never gave it back. Almost 40 years later, before the Virginia Rail's final fall from grace, the man's son sold it to a collector for $5,000 and told the old family story to a reporter, who promptly printed it in the Richmond paper. The company lawyers wouldn't let him use Blanchard Penn's name, though, once it was determined that she was still alive and living in Richmond.

Blinking in the welcome daylight of freedom, Blanchard ran to Neil and threw her arms around him.

"You are my prince, come to save me," she whispered to him. "I have to find some way to thank you." And she kissed him on the lips, inserting her inquisitive tongue into his mouth.

Neil never told her what he'd paid for her release. He just wanted to get back to Penns Castle, back to the store, where he was already overdue.

"You don't have to thank me," he said. "I don't even know why I did it."

"Please don't leave. You're all the family I've got. You mean all the world to me."

Neil pointed out the obvious, that she was the only child of two very wealthy parents.

"They'll never forgive me. For Jimmy. I see it every time one of them looks at me."

Neil doubted that this was true, and he tried to convince Blanchard that nobody in his right mind could hold her responsible for that.

They sat, silent.

Then, Blanchard asked him to take her back to Penn's Castle.

"The place or the town."

"The place. My home. Our home."

"It sure as hell ain't my home. I doubt if James Penn would say it was my home."

"It's as much yours as anybody's."

She took his right hand in both of hers.

"Let's go, Neil. Let's go out there. I haven't even seen the place since we moved last year."

Neil didn't know why he did it, although he wonders if he was guilty of baser motives than a desire to make Blanchard Penn happy one last time.

He called the store from a pay phone and apologized to Wade Ramsey, told him that a friend was in serious trouble and that he would make it up to Wade the next day.

"Why did you do it?" he asked Blanchard on the way out of town.

"I don't know. Something told me to do it. Something is always telling me to do stuff."

He couldn't tell if she was serious or not. He wasn't sure he wanted to know.

"Well, you know one of these days I won't be here."

"It was fate, don't you think, that you were here this time?"

Neil said he didn't know much about fate. He was more of the make-your-own-luck school.

"Take me out there," she said. "Please. I'll make it worth your while."

"I'm not sure I want you to make it worth my while," he told her.

Neil Beauchamp knew exactly what Blanchard was offering, as much as he tried to deny it to himself later.

"Oh," she said, running her left hand high up his inner thigh, almost making him run the red light at which they were stopped, "I think you do. Don't you?" And she ran her hand even higher.

And so Neil drove Blanchard Penn back to the castle where they both started their lives.

When they got there, Neil had to park alongside the road, because a chain barred the driveway. The house itself was locked, and Neil wouldn't let Blanchard break one of the windows.

"Haven't you done enough mischief for one day?" he asked her.

"Well, come on, then," she said, taking his hand.

They went around the house, to the back of the yard. To the gazebo, almost obscured by the weeds growing around it.

It was not a particularly cold day, but it was mid-February. Neil was comfortable enough in his jacket. Blanchard was wearing a tartan skirt and white blouse, with a cashmere sweater over the top.

No one could see them, but it still was as stunning to him as anything so far in his young life when she reached underneath her skirt and — she was not wearing stockings — slid her panties down to her ankles and then off, handing them to him.

"This," she said, "is your payment, kind sir."

He took the panties, slipping them into his pocket.

"Now," she said, moving closer to him and reaching for his zipper, "why don't you do something nice for both of us? Like fuck me."

Neil had never heard a woman say that word.

Neil Beauchamp never admitted it, but he was, that Valentine's Day, a virgin. Blanchard Penn, he soon came to understand, was not. She straddled him on the swing in her family's abandoned gazebo that February afternoon. She rocked the swing sideways, riding Neil until he had come three times. She whispered into his ear, "I'm never going to let you go."

Blanchard Penn was as beautiful as any 15-year-old in Richmond that year. She had sky-blue eyes and a face in which baby fat had been burned down to aristocratic lines. Her full lips were almost erotically pink. She was stylish and worldly far beyond 15. She flirted capably with grown men and was the wet dream of boys her own age. The occasional "zone" was seen not as a sign of insanity but as part of the general otherness that made Blanchard Blanchard. And she hadn't really had a bad spell in years, that anyone knew of.

Neil Beauchamp leaned back on the arm of the old swing and looked up at her while he stroked her ample breasts through the soft fabric and the bra underneath. He moaned her name and thought desire could not go beyond this without the risk of permanent injury.

Indeed, he could not swear to you now, with his sexual life a wilting flower, that his erotic pleasure ever exceeded that sunny afternoon on the slope beyond Penn's Castle, in the embrace of his half-sister, with a crow mocking them from a dead poplar tree in the field below.

When they were through, the post-coital cold and the shame almost made him want to cry. In spite of Blanchard's kisses, he had seldom felt more alone.

In his lust, he had not even thought about protection. He had carried a prophylactic in his wallet, had carried it for so long that it had left a circular bulge in the fabric, but it had not even occurred to him to put it on. By the time he thought to do so, it was too late to stop.

He was too embarrassed to mention this to Blanchard. Later, from her letters he received in Florida, he surmised that protection was the last thing she had wanted that day. But she did not get pregnant. Neil had, of course, never seen a woman achieve orgasm before, and he only realized, when he had a basis for comparison, that what he saw that afternoon in the Virginia woods went beyond passion and into what the Penns knew as a zone.

He left two days early for spring training, and he made it a point, for many years, to avoid situations where he might be alone with Blanchard Penn. They "stayed in touch," never going more than half a year without a call or a letter, more often from Blanchard than from Neil.

"You know," she finally told him, years later when she was living in New York and he was playing for the Cleveland Indians, in town for a four-game series, "you're the only man I ever wanted. You broke my heart."

Her second husband was sitting beside her, across the restaurant table, and he laughed as if he'd just heard the funniest joke in the world.

David has had time to read two of Blanchard's poems when he hears them coming in the back door.

He puts the album away, as close as he can to the way he found it. It's too late to escape the library undetected, so when they discover him, he is browsing, looking through a first edition of an early Dreiser novel when they come to the door.

"Well," Blanchard says, "isn't this a mess?"

"It's wonderful," David tells her. "I'd kill to have a collection like this."

"See anything you like, take it." She waves her arm to include the whole musty room.

David tells them the car is not ready yet, and excuses himself to make a phone call.

He catches Carly at home.

"I've got some bad news," he tells her. "They won't be able to fix the car until Friday morning. Something about a part that they can't get until then. Whatever. You know me and cars. I don't imagine this is what you want to hear, but I think I'd better stay down here, just have Thanksgiving with my father and his family tomorrow. Be a shame to have to come right back Friday morning."

Carly understands. Part of David wishes she wasn't quite so understanding. He speaks to both their daughters, assuring them he'll be home before they know it.

"Carly," he says, when she takes the phone again, "We're going to get through this. I swear. I love you."

"I know," she says. "Me, too."

She sounds tired.

Back in the living room, David tells his father and Blanchard that the garage has done it again, that they won't be able to fix his car until Friday morning.

"Do you think they'll have room for one more at Millie and Wat's tomorrow?" he asks them.

FIFTEEN

AT FIRST, NEIL doesn't hear the knocking. His ears aren't what they once were.

When he opens the door, slightly and with trepidation, David is standing there.

"What's the matter?" he asks his son.

"Nothing. I just wanted to ask you something."

It has been a quiet evening. After dinner, Blanchard put half a dozen jazz CDs on shuffle mode, and she and David drank half a fifth of bourbon while Neil sipped two colas. Blanchard told David stories about his father as she remembered him, with Neil only occasionally correcting her.

She did not offer to bring out any scrapbooks, though.

By 10:30, Neil could hardly keep his eyes open, and when he excused himself, the other two got up, a little unsteadily, to go to bed as well.

"Don't let me spoil the party," he told them.

"What fun is it to talk about you if you aren't here to embarrass?" Blanchard asked him, her words only slightly slurred.

"Well, I could tell him later," David said, but they were all tired.

"What?"

Neil, standing before his son in the old-man's boxer shorts and T-shirt he brought from Mundy, wants nothing less than a little heart-to-heart. Even when he and Kate were happily married, a condition that he believes existed for the majority of their wedded time, he was marked down for not being more open.

He thinks, now, that nothing in his life ever prepared him for openness, not his first life as Jimmy Penn, or his second as Neil Beauchamp, or his third, as the Virginia Rail. In the worlds in which he lived, people in general and men in particular bore joy and anguish in relative silence. They did not bare their souls. They most certainly did not cry.

Only in prison, when he had too much time to consider his life, did he concede that he might not have taken the most prudent course in the area of human emotions. By then, though, he was prone to agree with a fellow inmate who attached himself to Neil for some reason, a mostly toothless day-laborer who had cut up his foreman over some real or imagined slight. "You can lead a horse to water," the cellmate had said, "but you can't teach a old dog new tricks." The man advised Neil on many aspects of life, apparently being one of those souls who can solve others' problems but not their own. "You got to take it slow, enjoy life," he told Neil one day not long before Neil was likely to be paroled. "You got to stop and smell the coffee."

"What." David repeats the word as if it embodies all that has stood between them: What do you want now? What's the matter? What's so important that you have to disturb me? What's the use in talking?

"This is what: I want to talk to you. You're my father, for Chrissake, no matter how much you might want to deny it. We ought to talk."

He is leaning against the door frame, and Neil can smell the liquor, one of the disadvantages of not drinking any more himself.

"Ah, David," he turns his head from his son and walks a few steps into the room, finally sitting down on the end of the big bed, its spread still undisturbed and quarter-bouncing tight from when he made it this morning.

"I've never wanted to deny being your father," he says, when he is seated, looking up at David. He is tired enough that he feels about half-drunk himself. "I've always been proud of you. You did things I never would have been smart enough to do. You've made me and your mother proud."

David is standing in front of Neil, his hands in his pockets.

"Do you know, you've never said that before?"

Neil is sure he has, somewhere. He just can't remember when, and he doesn't feel like arguing.

"I'm sorry," he says, and he thinks back to all the times he said that to Kate, in the bad times, after Neil Beauchamp could no longer do the one thing God had made him to do. And how much it galled him, until he finally quit saying it — or anything else much — to the woman he once loved so dearly.

There were many good years, though, before all that. Neil can't deny it. He doesn't think he has any valid reason to complain. The way he sees it, some people get the good things early, and others get it late. Both have their advantages. And some don't have any good times at all, just one unbroken sea of crap from birth to merciful death. He learned that well enough at Mundy. But nobody, in Neil's experience, gets to have it good from start to finish. For him, the bad, what he's come to think of as The Time of Letting Go, came late, after everyone, including Kate, stopped cheering.

Detroit was the best. He led the league in hitting two times in a row, and he was an all-star almost every year. Neighborhood children would hang around his and Kate's house, hoping he might come out and talk with them, maybe even engage in a little game of catch. Later, he couldn't help wishing his own son wanted to play with the Virginia Rail as much as strangers' kids once did.

And then, the first season in Cleveland, he won a third batting title. He figures that was the one that put him over the top later, got him in the Hall of Fame the fifth year he was eligible, by four votes.

He sent money home to Penns Castle, long after it had stopped being "home" any more. He was liked by players and fans alike. He was adored by the beautiful Kate Taylor Beauchamp. He was a glittering adornment for her well-to-do family. Much later, he would understand that they had only known him when he was The Rail, and that neither he nor they were much enamored of the insecurity and emptiness and plainness that would outlive his ability to hit a baseball.

Neil told people that his hitting paid for the meal, and his fielding took care of the tips. He was dogged but uninspired at third base, then left field and first base. At the very end of his career, they changed the rules, and he had a chance, briefly, to play the position for which he was born: designated hitter. He didn't even have a glove.

A columnist in Cleveland wrote that Neil Beauchamp had everything it took to reach 3,000 hits. "He's got speed," the newspaperman wrote, "and he's got power when he wants to use it, although it seems sometimes that he'd rather drill a double into the gap in right-center than knock one over the fence. And he takes care of himself. He's here for the long haul."

But then Neil stepped into a drainage hole chasing a foul ball one day in Baltimore, in 1966, and by the time he had rehabilitated his knee, he was suddenly 32 years old, doomed to be merely good for a while, and then not even that.

He would later read an autobiography, when he was in prison, approximately the fifth book he had ever read that wasn't assigned to him. The mildewed library, smelling of bad food from the kitchen next door, had a very limited selection, depressingly top-heavy with religious tracts and romance novels that were donated by churches and discarded by real libraries. One day, alone with nothing but his thoughts, Neil went down there, and he found a book written by a man who also made the Hall of Fame, one of Neil's peers. The man was one of baseball's all-time home run leaders, and in the book, he admitted that, at a point in his late 20s, when power was overtaking speed, he had determined that he was going to stop swinging level, stop going for the hard singles and the doubles and triples in the gaps. He was going to hit home runs.

"All the guys getting the headlines were the sluggers, the home run guys," he or his ghostwriter explained. "I realized that they were getting all the endorsements, all the attention, and all the money.

"So I said, screw singles. I lost 30 points off my batting average, and I made more money. Everybody loves home runs."

Neil could relate. He never hit more than 27 home runs in one season, and that came late in his career.

He knew that the old-time slugger who said home run hitters drive Cadillacs and singles hitters drive Fords was right.

Still, he couldn't do it.

From the very beginning, he had felt there was a way to play baseball, a way to hit. Changing would have been a kind of betrayal. He had a swing, one that no manager or coach or scout ever taught him, and he thought that to alter that swing for the sake of money or fame (and he already had as much fame as he wanted) was unnatural.

One day, his last season with the Tigers, late in the season when the pennant race was a foregone conclusion, lost again to the inevitable Yankees, a teammate of his, a rookie, started riding him.

The rookie was one of those men Neil would see all through his big-league career, a one-trick pony who could hang well for a season or two but would eventually be undone by an inability to learn the pitchers' weaknesses as quickly and as well as they learned his.

That one year, though, the kid was on fire. By late August, he already had 26 home runs, with a chance for the American League rookie record. His last name was Brown, and he was, for that one season and a little bit of the next, Downtown Brown from Motown. Not only did he hit a lot of home runs, but he hit them deep, most going 400 feet or more, into the upper deck of Tiger Stadium or bouncing off its facade.

"Hey, Rail," he said to Neil in the locker room one day. "Rail! I got a hundred dollars says I get more home runs from here on out than you do all year."

It was a hot, humid day, and they were getting ready to play a twi-night doubleheader, something only the younger players had any zeal for at all.

A couple of the other rookies laughed. To the players nearer Neil's age, Brown was already wearing thin. Rookies, even at that late date, did not so freely throw around veterans' nicknames, and they didn't bait them.

Neil just smiled and shook his head, went back to autographing the box of baseballs in front of his locker. He had, so far that year, hit only 14 home runs.

"C'mon, Rail," the rookie said. "I know those old arms of yours are getting too tired to hit home runs now. Let me get some of that big old salary of yours. I know I can take you."

The rookie was smiling, but no one missed the challenge.

"Hey, Brown," a veteran relief pitcher said. "Why don't you shut the fuck up?"

This only served to ratchet the rookie up a notch. Neil refused to acknowledge him except to shake his head and smile again, and Brown went back to his locker, where he held court loudly enough for Neil to pick up most of what he was saying. Most of it was about the problems of having to "carry this friggin' team myself. Nobody's got any spirit here."

After five minutes of it, and understanding that nothing but some kind of confrontation would settle matters, Neil walked across the room and stood over the rookie, who was reading a comic book with his back against his locker.

"Tell you what."

"What?" The rookie put down the comic book.

"It won't be too good if we spent the rest of the season doing nothing but trying to hit home runs. How about this instead: I've got five hundred dollars says that I can hit more home runs than you by the end of the day. Either one of us gets benched, it's off."

"By the end of the day? You mean just one day?"

"That's it," Neil said. "One doubleheader. Five hundred dollars. Easy money."

Five hundred dollars was almost two months' rent in the apartment complex where all the rookies lived. Neil could see Brown swallow. He knew he could hit two home runs for every one the Virginia Rail could hit. Still, he hesitated. Maybe, Neil thought later, it was an inability to play better when the stakes were higher that finally did Downtown Brown in.

"OK, you got it, Rail," the rookie said, and they shook hands on it.

They were playing Minnesota that day. In the first game, Brown struck out twice and flied out twice, once to the warning track. Neil Beauchamp lined two home runs into Tiger Stadium's upper deck, the first time he'd homered twice in one game in almost two years.

Between games, Brown complained about the heat, about the lefthander that Minnesota had thrown at them, who must be scuffing the ball to throw such curves, about the difficulty of playing an afternoon game in such godawful heat.

"Well, Brown," the Tigers' catcher said, between sips of a 16-ounce beer that had chilled in a tub during the first game, "the second one, it'll be night again. And the Twins are throwing a righthander. You're bound to catch up."

There was general laughter, and Neil regretted being baited into the bet, because he knew that Downtown Brown, a building block for whatever future the team might have, might have fouled his nest in Detroit that one day, with a combination of hubris and panic. He had, he knew later, made Brown doubt his invincibility.

The second game went much as the first had. Brown, swinging mightily, dribbled a single between short and third, and he hit another ball to the warning track. Neil homered in the third inning, then was happy enough to sit for the last three.

By the time they got back in the locker room, having swept the Twins 9-3, 5-3, the clubhouse man had already found from somewhere a piece of cardboard, on which was written: Rail 3, Brown 0.

Downtown Brown tore the sign to pieces and did not speak to Neil for the rest of the season. He paid Neil his five hundred dollars on the last day, after much harassment by his teammates. He brought in 500 one-dollar bills and dumped them in Neil's locker while he was taking batting practice. After the game, Neil's teammates helped him collect the bills and put them in piles of 50, more or less.

But Neil knew, even if his teammates or his manager didn't, that he was not meant to swing for the fence every night. He had seen others have that rare two-homer night, or just hit one far into the lights, and fall in love with the sound of the bat and the way the whole stadium rained its temporary love on the man who could knock the ball a country mile. He had seen the diminishing returns, the loss of the sweet, straight whip of a swing. He had seen the .300 hitter with a little power become a .240 hitter with not much more.

"I've got a line-drive swing," he told his manager after he had won his bet with Downtown Brown. "If I start swinging for the fence, it won't work. It might for a while, but not forever."

The manager thought to say to Neil that nothing lasts forever, anyhow. But then he thought again, and just, as he said to one of his coaches, "let the Rail be the Rail."

He tells David the story of Downtown Brown.

"Yeah," David says when Neil goes silent. "I know how you felt about those home runs. I turned down a Washington p.r. job one time, flacking for a 'health-care provider.' 'Health-care depriver' was more like it. It would have paid almost twice what I was making at the paper. And, I'd probably still be employed. But I don't think I'd be very happy."

Neil nods. He supposes it is a good comparison, but he wonders how anyone could ever love newspaper work the way he loved baseball.

"What was it like?" David begins and then hesitates, lost in this unexplored territory. "I mean, between you and Mom? I mean . . . Shit, what happened?"

Neil looks at him.

"Hell, son, you were there. You know what happened."

"No, I don't. I mean, I thought everybody's parents fought sometimes. And I was gone before it got very bad."

David was only five when the Tigers traded his father to Cleveland, in 1964. He grew up in the suburbs there, except for two junior-high years, while Neil was ending his career in

Kansas City. When Neil took a job managing a Rookie League team in east Tennessee, Kate and David stayed in Cleveland.

Neil doesn't think, now, that Kate ever meant to be unkind, just as he never meant to hurt her. But he knew, as he saw his batting average fall, as he started lying awake in the predawn hours trying to imagine a bearable life that did not include playing baseball, that Kate's love was, after all, conditional.

Well, he supposes that his was, too. When his performance fell to a point at which Kate no longer treated his life as the sun around which hers and David's revolved, he turned cold, too. He drank, he strayed, he cursed.

The day Kansas City released him, in the summer of 1973, he was 30 pounds over his rookie weight, no rail by anyone's standards. With twice-cut-upon knees, he could hardly run at all. Even his sweet swing had turned sour. He had finally, in desperation as his reflexes lost another hundredth of a second, changed his batting stance, and by August, he was lost, a designated hitter who could no longer hit.

The general manager broke it to him. Neil had tried to imagine The End, when he could bear to look at that certainty straight on, but when the man across from him in the big office started talking about "new directions" and "other teams out there," all Neil could do was sit and nod dumbly. He caught his own reflection in the glass of a print behind the GM's head. The print was of a painting Kate had — he was sure — told him about once in a museum. Neil still had on his uniform, leaving only the spikes in the locker room, and thought that his likeness very much resembled a little boy dressed in a little boy's clothes, far out of his present league.

They were in the middle of a homestand, so all Neil Beauchamp had to do was clean out his locker, put a bag of his belongings in the car, and drive to his and Kate's rented house in the Kansas suburbs. He did not say goodbye to a single teammate, in the same spirit in which he would later discourage visitors when he was in Mundy. Most of the Kansas City players didn't really know him very well, anyhow. They were all younger by then; he hadn't won a batting title in nine years. They didn't know or care about his .316 career batting average; they only knew that he hit a useless .235 that season.

When he got home, it was after one in the morning. By that time, Kate was not going to very many of the games. Neil, who was developing a taste for gin, worried sometimes that the bourbon seemed to be disappearing at an unhealthy rate in his absence.

In Cleveland, where he had friends, he would have just gone out drinking, come in at four or five and dealt with it in the morning.

In Kansas City, though, he felt alone.

He was relieved to see the bedroom light still on as he drove up.

But then, when he came into the room, he saw that the bad news had preceded him.

"Gus Marquette called," she said, and her arms were folded. "He said you got cut today.

"Neil, why didn't you tell me this was going to happen?"

He had not known himself that the end was upon him. He supposed that he had fooled himself, believing right to the end that he would wake up one day a .300 hitter again.

"Told you?"

"I mean, here we are in Kansas City, in this hole, and now we can't even stay here," and she started crying.

"Somebody'll pick me up," Neil told her, but even he doubted it, and the following weeks, and then the silent winter, bore that out.

He considered himself lucky, after he had gotten over the pain, that the Indians were willing to give him a job managing in the minor leagues, a chance to stay with baseball. They had saved some money, and Kate had inherited more.

As he stood in the bedroom doorway that night in Kansas City, though, Neil Beauchamp looked down at the woman who had idolized him a few years earlier and knew that his world, whose balance of power had been shifting slowly for some time, was now an alien place. And he wondered where and if he would fit in it.

In the dark, Kate was crying, and he wanted to cry himself. He tried to comfort her, reaching a big hand across her from behind, his body spooning to hers. But she stiffened and moved a few inches toward her side of the bed, and he was too proud to follow her with his own body, seeking, reassuring.

Neil Beauchamp knew nothing was ever going to be the same.

He thought that night that the bill had come due on his entire adult life. And he doubted that he could pay it.

SIXTEEN

NEIL IS SITTING in the dining room, carefully administering syrup to four pancakes that are fanned out on his plate like a hand of cards.

"Well, good morning," Blanchard says when David walks in, rubbing his eyes. "I thought you'd be sleeping late today."

"I couldn't. It was too quiet. Where are the piledrivers?" His smile is faint but almost straight-on.

"Even those sons of bitches take Thanksgiving day off," Blanchard says, and goes to make more pancakes. "But I don't."

Neil and his son look at each other. Neil shakes his head.

One summer in college, David worked with a construction crew whose job it was to lay the footings on which houses would be built. Sometimes it seemed fruitless; you couldn't even see what they had done once the house was under way. But the foreman told them, over and over, that nothing worked right if they didn't get the footings right.

David guesses that they might have been laying the footings last night.

They talked into the early morning hours about games and seasons long gone, about Mundy, about David and Carly and the girls, about what comes next. Nothing, though, about the photo album. The talk was so good, he and the Rail actually on the same wavelength for a while, that David did nothing to alter the temporary magic.

Blanchard comes back in and sees Neil dispensing syrup. He puts just enough out to spread a thin sheen on each pancake, and he is down to his last one. He hovers over the plate, his elbows to the side, as if to block anyone who might take his food.

"Jesus," Blanchard says, taking a spatula and slapping three more pancakes on Neil's plate, then taking the syrup and pouring until the cakes are almost floating. "You're not in there any more, Neil Beauchamp. You can have as much damn syrup as you want, honey."

"The last time I visited him," she says, turning to David, "you know what he said he missed? Pancakes. Pancakes with all the syrup in the world. And now he's afraid somebody's going to hit him or something if he eats them."

Her voice cracks, and she turns away.

Neil reaches over and puts his hand on her back.

"Give me a little time," he tells her. "I'll be OK. I'm just not used to all this."

Blanchard returns to the kitchen. She is baking sweet-potato pies as her contribution to dinner at Wat and Millie's.

"I hope that won't be too fancy to offend their tender sensibilities," she says.

She comes out twice more to make sure both Neil and David have enough breakfast, then excuses herself to "prepare for the bacchanalia."

The two men clear the table. While they are removing plates and putting away milk and orange juice and syrup, Neil asks his son about Kate. David doesn't remember his father asking about her before, ever. He must have, David thinks, and I just can't remember.

"Well, she's doing well," he says, choosing each word as carefully as any politician he ever interviewed. "She's back in Detroit . . . Jesus, you know that. Grosse Point Shores. I guess Warren's doing pretty well."

Neil nods his head. He knows where the former Kate

Beauchamp lives, and he is aware of her husband's name and status.

"I mean," he says, closing the refrigerator door and turning to face David, "is she well? Is she happy?"

David says she is well, well enough for 61, and he supposes she is happy, although she is not terribly happy with him at the present.

"She did it all," Neil says, looking off through medieval windows into the woods beyond. "She raised you, and she carried me. She would pick out my clothes and pack my suitcase. Wouldn't let me lift a finger in the kitchen. I could barely dress and feed myself without her.

"She just thought I'd amount to more, is all. Thought I could do more than play ball. She had high standards."

David leans against the kitchen counter and sighs.

"I hear that."

"Well," Neil says, "she has more reason to hope with you."

"Right. I'm 38. I'm out of a job."

"Been there," Neil says, and he and David make eye contact and begin to laugh, Neil quietly while he sits at the table, David so uncontrollably that he has to wipe tears from his eyes.

The Great Letting-Go was not an avalanche. It was more like erosion as soft, rootless soil gradually slid downhill into a creek.

The Virginia Rail, once he had made it known that he wanted to remain "a baseball man," spent two summers managing a team in a rookie league where the players were all less than 22 years old and the season lasted less than three months.

He would manage for six years total in the minor leagues. None of his teams ever finished higher than second, and he could not swear that he ever made one player better.

177

He'd seen managers and coaches, when he was a player, who had his particular problem. They once were great talents, but all their talent was either born to them or nurtured at some level beyond conscious thought.

A 19-year-old first baseman at Johnson City, that first season, asked Neil to help him with his swing after he had struck out three times in a row.

Neil would watch the first baseman swing, and then he would tell him to just swing level, get that hitch out, don't be too impatient. But he could not break down what he did to individual components, like taking a watch apart. He had never done that with his own swing, for fear that he could not put it back together.

"Just a nice, smooth, even swing," Neil told the boy, and walked off. The player was gone after the season ended.

Kate stayed home. She had moved with David back to Cleveland, and the first two years, it wasn't so bad. Neil was only gone for a little more than three months, and his wife and son visited him on three occasions, although Kate thought the conditions of a minor-league manager were appalling and tried, not for the first time, to get him to go see her father about a position with one of his car dealerships.

"He wants you to take it over some day," she told Neil, as she had told him before.

But all Neil could see was a 20-year wait, learning "the car business" from a man who once fawned over him and would now be his boss. It was pride, as much as anything, Neil knows now. He was a baseball man, he told Kate. That was all he knew.

But it was fear, too. Neil Beauchamp, for all Kate's coaching, was a high school dropout whose skills inside the white lines of a baseball field far outstripped anything he had to offer outside them.

Kate had always run things, right from that first impromptu date. Before, though, she spent her energy on ensuring that the Virginia Rail had a smooth, seamless world in which to hit baseballs. Now, she saw herself as a force to make a new Neil Beauchamp, one whose success at a game somehow translated into a larger world, one in which men wore suits instead of uniforms and achieved their victories with suavity and stealth.

"Just let me try one more season," Neil pleaded with her. "I can make it back. I'm a better manager than the pinheads I played for."

He had never, ever had to beg for anything when he was hitting .330, and despite his better instincts, it soured him.

The third year, he was to be the manager of a Class A team in Winston-Salem. It was a step up, he insisted to Kate, and she said that at this rate he'd be 80 by the time he was a big-league manager.

That May, David's high school team was in the regional playoffs. When it reached the finals, scheduled for a Thursday evening, Neil left the team in the capable hands of his third-base coach for two days and caught a Thursday morning flight to Cleveland.

David was a junior that year. He had managed, through determination and (he always suspected) the coach's belief that genes would eventually out, to become the starting second baseman. He was the weakest hitter in the lineup but a competent fielder. Neil had worked with him during the previous two winters more than he had in the past, having less need to attend to his own physical fitness.

The two of them, though, were never in harmony. David was far past the point where Neil could become part of his day-to-day life. The Virginia Rail didn't understand the music, didn't understand the hair, but mainly, as hard as he tried to conceal it, did not understand how his son could be as devoid of that one skill on which Neil Beauchamp had built his entire life: hitting a baseball.

As useless as Neil was to his rookie league players, he was more so to his own son. If one of them wasn't angry, the other was. Neil would fume about David's inability to "just swing straight, dammit. Get rid of that hitch." And when David did, for short stretches, make good contact with the batting-practice pitches he was throwing, Neil would compliment him and David would respond with sarcasm: "Oh, blessed day. I have pleased the Virginia Rail. My life is complete." And Neil would get angry again.

Off the field, there was less tension between them but even less to communicate.

If there was a beach weekend to veto, a report card to criticize, a curfew violation, it fell to Kate. Neil had come to believe, after so many years of absentee parenthood, that he did not even have the right any more to deal with his son except on a baseball field.

"Neil," Kate told him when he called to inform them that he would be flying in for the Thursday night game, "he's not ever going to be you. He's doing the best he can."

Neil said he knew that, that he just wanted to be there for his son.

Kate sighed, and said she wished sometimes that she had never allowed David to play baseball.

Neil hung up.

He arrived in Cleveland at three in the afternoon. The game was scheduled for six. Neil planned to meet Kate there. With a couple of hours to kill, he went to an airport bar, where two men his age recognized him immediately and began buying him beers.

Neil Beauchamp had, in the solitude of small summer towns, begun to drink more. He found that it smoothed the way between the games — which were played in tiny, aging confines of dying grass and rock-ruined infields that did not deserve the name "stadium" — and sleep, which was eluding him more and more.

Sometimes, he and the coaches would drink a case of beer among the three of them before calling it a night. So, Neil didn't suppose a few beers in an airport lounge would hurt much.

By the time he left, it was after five, and he had enjoyed six beers at the expense of people who he felt still admired him. He was jolted a little when he saw, out of a mirror in the bar as he left, one of the men look at the other and smile with what might have been indulgence or even sadness, but certainly was not giddiness over spending two hours talking baseball with the Virginia Rail.

It put an edge to whatever ebullience he had reached in the lounge, and he was more impatient than usual with the slow traffic of rush hour.

The national anthem was just concluding when he reached the park. There were no more than 300 people in the bleachers around home plate and down the baselines, and he found Kate quickly enough.

"You've been drinking," she said, and he said just a drink or two on the plane.

He remembered, later, being impatient when David struck out in the third and fifth innings. He remembered Kate shushing him and he remembered telling her, not too loudly, he was sure, to shut up.

Pitching dominated the game, and David's team trailed 2-1 going into the bottom of the seventh and final inning. The first two batters struck out, and people began collecting themselves to leave. But then a walk and a single to the team's only two competent pinch-hitters put runners on first and third, and it was down to David.

Part of Neil relished the moment, the way he himself had

in that long-ago high school game in Richmond, when he revealed himself to be a Talent. Part of him cringed, and he knew he had no faith in his son. He knew that what he really wished he could do was go up there himself and be the hero, one more time.

"Oh, my God," Kate muttered, and he knew she feared the worst, too.

There was no one left on the bench except a couple of ninth-graders and a boy whose foot was in a cast, and it looked to Neil as if the coach was seriously considering one of those three alternatives. Finally, though, he shrugged and motioned David toward the plate, which he approached with what looked like hesitation.

The pitcher seemed to be smirking, and Neil remembered how he had loved to wipe the arrogance off such faces.

The first pitch was dead across the plate, but David, hoping for a walk, watched it. Neil knew it was the best pitch his son would see.

The second pitch was low and away. David, daring not let a second called strike go by, and not having his father's quick and discerning eye to judge a pitch between the pitcher's hand and the catcher's glove, swung wildly and missed.

"Oh, no," Neil groaned, and Kate elbowed him.

The third pitch was a cruel curve that came in knee-high and broke into the strike zone. David watched it, and the game was over.

He argued with the umpire, but not even his coach backed him up, and when David turned around to walk toward the bench, they were already packing up the equipment.

"Neil," Kate said as they stood, taking his arm, "please don't make him feel any worse than he already does."

And Neil really did not mean to make his son feel worse. He really did love David. He always had. But he was so disappointed. Despite David's good grades and at least passable looks and personality, Neil felt the boy had to prove himself, at some point. He had to step up to something or someone better than he was and beat that thing or that person, if he was ever going to succeed.

They waited for their son at Kate's car, saying little to each other. David was supposed to be going somewhere afterward with his teammates, in his newly-acquired, well-worn Plymouth, but he'd said he would come by to say hello to his father first.

Neil had a Saturday morning flight south, where he would rejoin his own team after a day with his family. David was taking Friday off from school. Maybe they could go to the lake, to the park they used to go to sometimes, where Neil could remember them being happy together.

But David told them he thought he'd just go home, that he'd see them there later.

"Why don't you go out with your teammates?" Neil asked him.

"Because I don't want to."

Kate tried to usher Neil away. He had never taken the time to learn when to be silent, never learned the rhythms of teenage stages.

But Neil moved away from her, toward David.

"You've got to get right back in there," he said, not sure he knew what he meant but feeling he had to say something. "You can't let some candy-ass high school pitcher get the best of you. We'll go out tomorrow . . ."

David, who had his back to his father, wheeled around, and Neil could see his eyes shining.

"You'd better remember this night, Rail," he said — he seldom called Neil "dad" any more. "This is the end of a great career, the end of an era. You've seen the last appearance of David Beauchamp, Son of Rail. Career batting average, .125. Good field, no hit, no chip off the old block."

"You've just got to try harder . . ."

"No! I don't have to try harder. I don't have to do anything. I don't have to ever pick up a baseball again, and I'm not going to."

He spun and walked away. Neil grabbed him.

"Okay, then. Go ahead and be a quitter." The word stuck in his throat, but he plunged on into the dark. "You embarrassed me tonight. Who the hell taught you to hit like that?"

David walked on, toward his new-old car. Kate had at first tried to stop Neil, tugging on his arm to quiet him. A small crowd, the remnants of the game's spectators, was watching and listening.

Then she let go, and she, too, turned away from him. Neil was left standing by himself in the asphalt parking lot, watched from a distance by strangers who recognized him.

"I'll see you at home," he said, and Kate said, "No, you won't."

When Neil drove the rental car into their driveway, the house was dark. He waited inside for an hour, but neither his wife nor his son appeared that night.

He stayed in a motel, unable to bear the brick rancher by himself. He was able to change his flight the next morning after calling the house twice and getting no answer.

Over the months and years, he and Kate and David would patch things up, but the wounds underneath got no air and didn't really heal.

David kept his promise and never played another game of baseball. Neil never asked him to.

One more year, and David was out of high school, gone to Ohio State, with summer jobs, first in construction and then interning at daily newspapers in other parts of the country. It seemed to Neil that he chose the jobs that would take him as far as possible from home.

It was easy enough for the Virginia Rail to stay employed in baseball, although the jobs that had either real money or real clout always seemed to go to someone else, someone who had gotten his college degree in the off-seasons or someone who could teach because, lacking Neil Beauchamp's natural talent, he had been forced to learn.

Neil spent summers in Salinas and Chattanooga and Buffalo, then four seasons as a base coach for Seattle and Texas.

The marriage wouldn't come completely apart until the summer of 1983, the year after he and Kate traveled to Cooperstown for the culmination of Neil Beauchamp's life achievements, his induction into baseball's Hall of Fame. Neil remembers that they argued back at the motel that night, something about his drinking too much.

He and Kate had been as separated as a married couple could be, and Neil couldn't even really remember when they became separated. He would go away every summer, and every summer he and Kate found fewer reasons to get together for occasional weekends. Their sex life, once a wet, lush entity, had dried up, and Neil added occasional women to his road vices, although he never felt a pull toward any of them that lasted longer than sexual fulfillment. In the winter, they had some good moments, and David would always come home for Christmas, first from college and then from jobs at small newspapers. They argued, but mostly they left each other alone.

In the summer of 1983, Neil came back to Cleveland at the All-Star break, not really planning to spend his three days off with Kate, who didn't know he was coming. Instead, he had decided that it was time to confront the rumors he had heard, second- and third-hand, that Kate Beauchamp had taken up with a relief pitcher for the Indians, a man 20 years younger. He didn't completely discount it; Kate was still a fine-looking woman, firm of body and face, "a tough-minded broad," as Neil had heard one of his old teammates refer to her.

Still, as much as he suspected the worse, when he got there and saw how it was, he was undone. There was a new black Corvette in the driveway, blocking him, forcing him to park on the street. The pitcher's clothes were in his closet, pushing his to the back corners. Neil's picture was missing from the bedside table. A beer, not his brand, was stocked in the refrigerator.

They were gone somewhere. Neil drank one of the relief pitcher's beers. Then he walked out the kitchen door to the garage, where he found the gasoline for the lawnmower. He poured gas in front of the Corvette and watched it flow underneath the body of the car. He went back and found the kitchen matches. On his way out again, he stopped where the drive ran into the street, where the gas had stopped running, and he lit one match and threw it down.

By the time he had started his own car and was edging out into the street, the Corvette was more or less consumed.

She called him the next day. He told her that he wanted a divorce, which was a lie, but he had no choice, he felt. He knew people "patched things up," but he had never learned much about healing, and he figured she had enjoyed as much of the Virginia Rail as she could stand, anyhow.

For some reason, she never mentioned the Corvette to him.

The pitcher was gone when the season ended, and by November, Kate Taylor had moved back to Detroit.

By then, Neil Beauchamp, fired with the rest of the Texas staff at the end of a dismal season, was at long last out of baseball, unable to endure another bus season in Rochester or Wichita, unwanted in the big leagues, unskilled labor.

SEVENTEEN

BLANCHARD IS WEARING a black dress that shows off her still-fine figure and not-yet-faded tan. Neil doubts that she has gained a pound in all these years. She might even have lost weight since her New York days. She has used makeup and lipstick to maximum advantage.

David turns from his conversation with Neil and whistles appreciatively. She kisses him on the cheek.

"Somebody better get moving," she says. "We've got to be over there by one-thirty, two at the latest."

There's only enough hot water for one shower at a time. Neil insists that David go first.

After he's left the room, Blanchard looks over to the table where Neil is sitting. From somewhere, he's gotten a pencil, and he seems to be scribbling numbers on a piece of scratch paper, lost in thought.

She walks over and leans down, pulling his face to hers, and kisses him on the lips, slipping her tongue into his mouth. He can taste her perfume and the taste beneath that, still familiar to him.

He tries to push away, scraping the chair backwards across the floor, but he feels the pull, too, and it takes him several seconds to escape.

"Blanchard," he says, leaning to pick up the pencil. "Don't."

"Have you told him?" she asks, her eyebrows rising as she looks up at him.

"Told him?"

"About us. Of course, I don't suppose you need to. Oh, it's going to be grand, Neil."

Neil leans back against the sink.

"Blanchard . . ."

But she is walking swiftly toward the back of the house.

"Cully! Here, boy!" She opens the door and starts whistling.

Neil comes up behind her. He puts his hands on her shoulders.

"Blanchard. Come on back. Come on now."

When she turns around, it's as if none of it happened.

"Well," she says, "I guess we'd better start getting stuff gathered up. Can you put some tinfoil around these pies, Neil? Do you want something to drink? Damn, I could use something."

Neil doesn't even know why she's doing it. He's looked in the mirror enough, as much as he tries not to, and he knows what two years in Mundy, plus all the wasted ones before, have done. Who would want him?

When they're seated at the table, her with her first bourbon-and-water of the day, him with a glass of orange juice, she looks over at him, more clear-eyed now that she has drained a long drink.

"Neil," she says, "I've got to make it right. I want to make it right. I owe you."

"You've taken me in," he tells her. "But that's all, OK? I can help around here. I'm not afraid to work."

"I'm not taking you in. He gave this place to you, too. It's yours as much as mine. But you know how it is."

She shrugs her shoulders, and then she's shaking, crying, her makeup and lipstick smearing.

He does know how it is, wonders how it is that some things and some people don't change. He's gotten over a lot. He hardly even thinks of Kate now. But Blanchard hangs on to everything.

Neil picks up the Richmond paper. There, on the bottom of the front page, is a story about a prison that the state is almost ready to open, built much farther back in the hills than Mundy, even. According to the story, the new prison is on top of a strip-mined mountain, with the possibility of a view stretching for miles.

Someone in the corrections department, though, worried that the inmates would be unworthy of such beauty, and so the glass is to be tinted and distorted. They will only be able see the ridges beyond their world the way a person with cataracts might.

Neil supposes a prisoner might derive some contentment or peace, maybe even false hope, from such unreachable scenery.

As for himself, he doesn't remember ever thinking to take the long view, if one even existed, during his time at Mundy. One minute, one hour, one day, one week, one foot in front of the other: That was how he got by. His only hope was that he would live to see a world where he might be able to hope again.

He was there for 23 months. At the sentencing, the judge told him he could have gotten 10 years for vehicular manslaughter, along with the drunk driving and the other charges, but no one could remember a longer sentence being meted out to the guilty party in a DWI fatality.

His lawyer told him beforehand that being a celebrity could work for or against him, that they might go easier because he was the Virginia Rail, or they might go harder, because he was the Virginia Rail.

It did not help Neil that he already had one DWI charge in the previous two years.

The late Lacy Haithcock's father was quite eloquent, and there was a double line of state troopers sitting grimly, creased hats held in clenched fists.

The judge, a man Neil's age, had iron-gray hair slicked straight back in lines like prison bars. By the time he arrived at his sentence, even Neil Beauchamp accepted it as inevitable and fitting for such a crime.

He said he was sorry, that he wished he could bring Lacy Haithcock back.

"But you can't," the judge said, and he looked sad.

There was talk that they might send a baseball Hall-of-Famer to a country-club prison, but Mundy was no country club. It was not hell, Neil supposed, but it was close enough.

They strip-searched him when he arrived and then almost blinded him with disinfectants. He could hear the guards laughing; they were mostly ignorant younger men, almost all of them white. They didn't know exactly who he was except that he was one of the mighty whom the gods dropped into their grasp on occasion, for their amusement.

They took everything he wore in, returning it to him nearly intact almost two years later, long after he had forgotten he'd ever worn brightly colored shirts and pants with creases and shoes that shined. He found, dressing himself the morning David was to pick him up, that he had nearly forgotten how to tie a shoelace.

He spent two weeks in "seclusion," because there was a rumor that someone might hurt him, for some reason. Most of the time, though, he shared a 12-by-14 cell with from one to three other men. They tried, in what seemed an uncharacteristic act of kindness, to keep the older prisoners together.

His pillow was a worn, folded-up blanket. He became accustomed to the cockroaches, the infested, inedible food, and the stench of shit and piss from backed-up toilets. He learned to sleep through the screaming, learned to look the other way. He had grown more garrulous in the letting-go years, but in prison he learned again the beauty of silence, the ugliness of talk to which he contributed only enough so as not to seem "above" the rest. In truth, he never felt above anyone at Mundy.

The first week, he realized later, he was in shock, sleep-walking through it all. Then, the days started their ivy-slow creep. The time from breakfast until lunch was longer than any of his free days had been.

After a month or so, they let him have pencil and paper. He did not write often, and then usually to Blanchard, his only visitor. He had made it clear to everyone, when he knew what lay ahead, that he wished to be among the dead at least until he was released.

There were times when he wished that everyone except Blanchard — his other sisters and brother, his son, his ex-wife, his former friends and acquaintances — had not taken him quite so literally, but that usually was on visiting day or in the middle of the night. Mostly, he knew it was for the best.

A reporter from the Detroit paper tried repeatedly to get him to submit to an interview; Neil finally wrote him, begging him to please leave him alone, which the reporter eventually did.

Neil had never been a reader or a writer. With the paper and pencil, though, and nothing else with which to distract himself except light work in the kitchen and the banalities of such social contact as was necessary, he turned to numbers.

He had been a good math student, or at least better than in other subjects. He had liked the hardness and sureness of numbers, as solid as a line drive past the pitcher's ear.

Now, he started playing mathematical games that he made up, scribbling constantly and then throwing the sheet of paper away. He would take numbers and square them, then cube them, subtract the square from the cube and compare the difference to the square and cube of the next-highest and next-lowest numbers. He would construct grids in which he squared numbers, then carried them to the third and fourth and fifth powers and beyond, then added up the horizontal, vertical and diagonal numbers, then subtracted them from each other, with no real motive other than to make what was in front of him, all around him, go away for a while.

He would do division and multiplication in his head, three numbers times three. He would figure batting averages and earned-run averages, work backward through the years to determine the day of the week Hiroshima was bombed, the day Lincoln gave the Gettysburg Address, or any of a thousand other events whose dates he got from a world almanac someone had donated to the library. He could tell you the day of the week on which his mother and his father were born. He would, finally, make up a date from centuries past and calculate the day of the week on which it fell.

Many around him, seeing him sitting on his bed or working in the prison kitchen with a faraway look, his lips moving slightly as he calculated some distant, meaningless sum, thought he might be losing his mind, but it was just the opposite. If anything kept him sane, he believes now, it was numbers. Their logic, cold and mysterious, would yield to him at unexpected moments some fact known by any college mathematics major but as amazing to Neil as an alien life-form.

Some men found such salvation as could be conjured up in the Bible or the Koran. Some found it in law books and the overblown, overly-optimistic appeals that sprang from them. Some found it in the weight room, or drugs.

For Neil Beauchamp, it was numbers.

Now that he's free again, he cannot tell you one single thing, useful or useless, that he learned in all his scribbling, all his figuring, except for the one, largest thing: how to make a nightmare world disappear, if only for a few minutes at a time.

The only time the sheer claustrophobia of it all got to him was in the final two months. Before that, even Blanchard's amazing news that he had inherited half of Penn's Castle, that James Blackford Penn had finally recognized his only living son, was not enough to faze him.

Neil knew of other men who had destroyed their chances for release with the open gates in sight, and some said it was because they couldn't deal with life on the outside. Neil, though, believes it is something else that makes men founder yards from the finish line. In the last two weeks, he realized that he was more jumpy, more irritable than before, unable to concentrate on his mind-saving numbers. He almost got into a fight with a prisoner half his age, over a piece of bread. Once he allowed himself to see a date, an actual day and hour of his possible release, he was unable to make himself not think about it, and the knowledge of what was there, almost within reach, made the 12-by-14 reality of his world almost unendurable.

He wonders what he might have done if he had not gotten his parole on the day he had allowed himself to hope he would get it, once he finally let hope crawl back into his life.

"The first time I saw you in there," Blanchard tells him, "I didn't think you'd last a month. You'd lost 20 pounds at least, and you looked like you were scared to death."

"I needed to lose some weight."

"Well, now you need to gain some back. And I'm going to help you. You've always looked after me, Neil. Now you've got to let me take care of you."

Neil looks up at her.

"Not always. There were lots of times I wasn't there."

She smooths his still-uncombed hair.

They hear David coming down the hall, and Blanchard is

at the refrigerator, looking for something, when he enters the room.

"Shower's all yours," he says. Neil rises stiffly and leaves.

"Do you think he's going to be OK?" David asks Blanchard after he hears the distant bedroom door close. "I mean, I could take him back up with me." He can't believe he's said it, can't really see how he could make it work if Blanchard called his bluff.

She turns from the open door.

"He'll be fine," she says, and there's an edge to her voice. "Don't you worry. He'll be taken care of here. He belongs at Penn's Castle."

EIGHTEEN

To DAVID, THE chaos at Wat and Millie's seems as practiced and expected as turkey and dressing.

All of the women except Blanchard, are in the kitchen, talking over each other and arguing about the thickness of gravy and the necessity of cranberry sauce.

The children — Ray and Patti's Rae Dawn and Susan's Sara and Ben — are watching the TV in Wat's den, from which Rae Dawn emerges every five minutes crying that she is being picked on.

Wat, Jack, Ray, David and Susan's boyfriend Parker are watching a pro football game in the living room.

Blanchard leans on the door frame leading to the kitchen, not quite in either orbit, sipping on a Coke enhanced by one of the mini-bottles of bourbon from her purse. She is watching Neil, who sits to one side of the small living room, facing the television but not joining in the sports banter around him.

The heat is stifling. It is a cloudy, temperate day, more like early October; it's at least 80 degrees inside. When Jack gets up during a commercial to go outside and get away from the cigarette smoke, David follows him to the cooler air.

Wat and Millie's porch is screened, looking out into a backyard of tan zoysia grass dotted with Bradford pears, pecan trees and crape myrtles.

"Hot," Jack says, and David agrees, breathing deeply and gratefully.

"So," Jack says, turning toward David, "how's he doing?"

"The Rail? Dad? Oh, he's fine. Just adjusting to real life again. It's going to take a while. At least he has a place to stay. Thank God for James Blackford Penn." David forces a laugh.

Jack is quiet. They both watch as two squirrels scurry along the branches of a pecan tree whose base is littered with ruined shells. David is about to make a comment about what a nuisance squirrels are, rats with tails, really, when a darkness passes in front of them. The red-tailed hawk is gone with the squirrel before they even know what it is. It becomes a speck against a gray sky in scant seconds. The other squirrel sits in the V of two branches, shaking and then scrambling as far up the bare tree as he can.

"Well, I'll be damned," Jack says, and he and David concede that they've never seen anything quite like that.

They compare other feats of nature they've witnessed, including Dasher.

Jack sets his Coke on the ashtray along the porch rail. Then he turns to David.

"I know the lawyer who drew up James Penn's will," he says, and David wonders what, if any, response is expected.

There is silence for a few more seconds. Jack Stoner speaks again.

"David, I don't know why I'm telling you this, except I can't keep a damn secret. The lawyer, he can't keep a secret either, I suppose, but he said he was just amazed when he heard what Blanchard was telling people. About the will."

"The will."

"David," Jack says, drawing him by the elbow away from the sliding glass door to the porch's far corner, as if they could be heard over the now-resumed game, "James Penn left everything — the house, whatever money was left, everything — to Blanchard. Neil got nothing, at least not from him. Nothing. He wasn't even mentioned."

David is looking across the yard, to the woods beyond. He thinks for an instant he sees a deer, but when he looks again, it is either gone or camouflaged.

"Nothing."

"Nothing. I don't know what it means, and I don't know why I'm telling you."

David turns back toward the house, fixing his gaze on Dr. Jack Stoner for two seconds.

"I don't either." And he goes back inside.

The house's population has grown by two while David was on the porch. Tom has arrived with a woman who appears to be about 10 years younger, a redhead wearing some kind of animal fur who looks as if she would rather be almost anywhere else.

Tom introduces her as Ella Turpin, and the others greet her pleasantly enough. She wants to stay close to Tom in this house full of someone else's family, and they settle in the middle area where Blanchard is trying to make her drink last as long as possible.

They finally sit down to dinner at 4:30, all 16 of them. Wat has had to add two leaves to the table, which stretches out of the dining room and into the adjoining den. They've put a card table in the den for the three children.

There is no seating plan, and they divide by generations. David joins Ray, Patti, Susan and Parker on the side of the long table nearest the children, with Willa, Jack, Tom, Ella, Blanchard and Neil on the other. Millie and Wat sit at either end.

They join hands. Wat asks God's blessing on the food before them and notes that he is thankful for family on such a day as this.

David looks across to where Neil is sitting with his head bowed, between Blanchard and Tom's girlfriend, Ella. He hasn't heard Neil say more than a dozen words since they arrived, and he imagines his father is just as happy not to be entertaining questions about the last two years. Everyone seems to prefer it that way. Blanchard's eyes are wide open, and they meet David's briefly before the blessing is concluded. She appears flushed.

When the blessing is over, Ella seems to have overcome her earlier shyness. She appears to be trying to draw Neil out, although David can't hear everything she's saying. Neil seems to be mostly nodding and answering as economically as possible.

The table is covered from one end to the other with turkey, ham, dressing, gravy, sweet potatoes, mashed potatoes, carrots, beans, field peas, biscuits, cranberry sauce, stewed tomatoes and squash. There are three casseroles.

Everything, David thinks, but a green salad. He feels as if he has gained five pounds already from his stay in Penns Castle, and he's liable to add another five before the day is over.

He and Carly agree that Thanksgiving feasts are a waste — all that food, she would lament, and everyone inhales it in 20 minutes. Then the men go back and fall asleep in front of a TV football game and the women clean it all up.

One year, the two of them tried to make it better. They invited six friends over and planned a five-course meal that they would eat, one leisurely course at a time. They would have a different glass of wine with each one, and when it was all over, everyone would have enjoyed a three-hour dining experience in which you actually tasted the food rather than simply swallowing it. It was all very French.

Their friends came, and for the most part they tried everything, remarking on how interesting everything was. After everyone left, David and Carly were quite proud of themselves and thought that perhaps they had broken new Thanksgiving ground. The next year, though, one of the other couples invited everyone over to their house, and there were the turkey, dressing, gravy, cranberries and all the rest, and no one mentioned the Beauchamps' ground-breaking meal of the year before. They ate everything in an enthusiastic 20 minutes, and although the men did help clear the table, it was not appreciably different from the holiday meals the eight of them had eaten when they were children. Everyone watched the rest of the football game together.

That was the point at which David and Carly stopped trying to improve on Thanksgiving.

"You can lead a guest to turkey terrine and sweetbreads," David told her on the way home that night, "but you can't make them eat."

It takes 10 long minutes for everyone to pass everything to everyone else, and then the table gets quieter as serious eating begins. Over Millie's protests, Wat has bought several bottles of passable Virginia wine, a merlot, and everyone except Neil fills a glass.

After a few quiet moments, Ella turns to Neil.

"So, Mr. Beauchamp," she says, "I understand you've been away at Mundy. My cousin's son is there. He was a fine boy, but he got mixed up with that crack cocaine."

The table grows quieter.

"Yes," Neil says, "I've been away."

David can see Tom's face redden as he tries to nudge his friend into silence. David wonders if Blanchard hasn't shared her cache of mini-bottles with Ella.

"Well, I reckon everyone else knows," she says gaily, "but what'd you do?" She giggles. Tom is looking down at his plate, his mouth full of food.

Neil chews a few more times and swallows.

"I was driving drunk and I ran over a man and killed him,"

Neil says, staring straight ahead, at a spot beyond Patti's head. Everyone is looking either down at their food or at Neil.

"Well," Ella Turpin says, "I guess that's why you're not having any wine."

"I guess so."

Susan gets up to go check on the children, and Patti follows her. Millie goes to get more turkey.

The quiet lasts until Wat says, "We were all sorry, Neil. We wished you'd have let us come see you. Hell, nobody blames you. Ain't been but one man that was perfect, and they nailed him to a cross."

Neil knows he's trying to make it better, trying to guide this holiday meal through uncomfortable shoals without making him feel like a total asshole. But he doesn't know what to say, other than, "Thank you."

It is Blanchard who gets up and leaves the table, her face pale and tight.

By the time she comes back, 10 minutes later, the other women have brought out the desserts — sweet potato pie, pecan pie, pumpkin pie, lemon pie, pound cake, German chocolate cake, angel food cake — and a certain equilibrium seems to have been reached. Ella is restricting her conversations mostly to Tom, and Susan's boyfriend is asking Neil about his glory days with the Tigers and Indians.

"You know," he said, as he lifted several ounces of pecan pie to his face, "I got your autograph once, when I was about six. You were out at the big card show they have every year. I've still got the ball you signed for me."

Neil nods. He autographed a lot of things, in a lot of cities, on his way to Mundy. After everything else went to hell, after the divorce finally came through and it was clear that he could not properly manage a baseball team, or a bar, or his half of a marriage, or even himself, it came down to signing things. He brought in more money on a slow July afternoon in Richmond signing scraps of paper and baseball cards, and caps and bats and gloves, than he made his first year with the Detroit Tigers.

"Yeah," Neil nods, looking across the table, "I signed a lot of balls back then."

Neil Beauchamp returned to Virginia the first time in 1985, the same year Blanchard came back. His plan was that he would start a sports bar in Richmond, which he would call simply The Rail.

He still had some money after the divorce and settlement, and he knew other ex-players who claimed a sports bar was an intelligent way to make money grow. And by this time, Neil had had some experience with bars. His partner was a developer who put up 60 percent to Neil's 40, since the developer had more money and considerably less name recognition.

Neil was, by then, well into The Great Letting-Go. He and Blanchard had never completely lost touch with one another. She would write to him occasionally as he went from minor-league manager to major-league coach to unemployed and divorced, and as she went through two marriages and a breakdown.

The developer also gave Neil a sweet deal on a condominium he had built in the Richmond suburbs. Having a Hall-of-Famer in one of his buildings could possibly help sales, the developer supposed.

They called the living spaces units. Neil had one with three bedrooms and a fireplace; it overlooked a creek 40 feet below. Every night at 11, the train would pass along the opposite bluff, its light visible through the oak and sycamore leaves. Neil sat up and listened for the train, came to expect its two long blasts as it neared the crossing half a mile up the tracks. He looked as expectantly as a child for its one-eyed, ghostly appearance, gliding through the woods exactly at his level, across the ravine.

Some nights, though, the Virginia Rail was not home to hear the train whistle. The condominiums were populated by retirees, young marrieds and what Neil's neighbor and fellow divorcee Pat McLean referred to as the At Large. Weber kettle grills would be lit at six, down by the two picnic tables that sat in front of Neil's unit, and the communal drinking would begin. On at least two occasions that Neil can remember now, no meat ever touched the grill's surface, and they all drove to The Rail for burgers, with Neil picking up the tab.

The sports bar lasted nearly three years. Neil had neither the patience nor the business acumen to be more than an occasional, drunken guest at the place that was draining his money. The man who would get up on the coldest winter mornings in Cleveland or Detroit in order to go to the gym and work out for two hours could not make himself rise to the call of commerce.

After the bar failed, it was back to Cleveland, where a man who was once an Indians bat boy offered him a great deal on a restaurant. This time, the name was less subtle: Neil Beauchamp's Hall of Fame Auberge. Later, after the bankruptcy papers had been filed, the former bat boy wondered if they shouldn't have called it a restaurant instead.

"People don't like that fancy shit," he said. Neil wished, as he had in Richmond, that he cared more.

Neil spent a decade moving, from Richmond to Cleveland, back to Richmond for a short spell, then to Kansas City and finally, in 1994, to Richmond again. After a while, he stopped unpacking certain boxes, and it seemed to him that he liked every place he lived a little less than the one before.

In Richmond, Blanchard would inevitably find him. No one else in his family tried very hard, and Neil had little heart for seeing them, ashamed that he could no longer send consistent small checks and occasional large ones, even though no one really needed the Rail's help any more. He would visit over Christmas, maybe once in the summer, if then.

He and Blanchard found that they were equally fond of drinking, and they would sometimes meet at bars in the Fan, or down in Shockoe Slip. Neil would be watching television in his apartment, and Blanchard would call, wanting to do something.

He was spending more and more nights by himself, and it was harder to turn down Blanchard's entreaties. He never came inside her big house in the West End, though. He never saw James or Virginia Penn in the years they had left.

"They think," Blanchard said to him once, when he was 57 and she was 52, "that you're a bad influence."

And when Blanchard would hint, and then outright ask, to come home with him, Neil always told her no.

In the year or so before the accident, she never even asked, and he assumed that the great, howling temptation that had always been there between them had at last, mercifully, become old and sickly, no longer scratching at his door, wanting to be let in as much as he wanted to let it in.

By 1994, Neil Beauchamp's sources of income were his baseball pension and the card shows. At the time little Parker's father paid ten dollars for Neil's name on a cheap baseball, he didn't need the money that much. After two bankruptcies, though, at a time when the Virginia Rail could have used the cash, he had been devalued to five dollars a ball. The more he needed money, the less he seemed to make.

The worst, he believes now, before the wreck, was when he did television commercials for what even Blanchard derided as loan sharks, trying to get people even more desperate than Neil to go deeper in debt for some short-term gratification.

He couldn't bear to look at the commercials when they came on. He would be standing there, looking almost as wooden as the bat he held on his shoulder.

"Can't get money?" he asked, and they'd had him do it at least 12 times to get the right emphasis in the question. "We'll go to bat for you. We'll drive home that new TV set, that new washer-dryer, that new car. We want to be on your team!"

Among the very few good things that came from his prison sentence was that they stopped running the commercial.

They are starting to drift away from the table now, the men looking for a place to collapse under dinner's weight, the women carrying half-eaten platters into the kitchen to be tinfoiled and stored for a week of leftovers.

Neil finally goes into the living room, where they make a place for him on the couch. In the middle of all these well-fed, good-natured men, he feels as much of a sense of camaraderie as he believes is possible. David is sitting across from him, and they exchange a smile.

Within 15 minutes, Wat Moseley is asleep in the recliner next to him, snoring lightly, and Neil's own eyes are getting heavy when he feels a hand on his shoulder.

"Here's the car keys," Millie says softly. "Blanchard said to tell you she had something to do, for you all to stay as long as you like. She said she'd just walk home."

It's only a quarter-mile walk, so Neil supposes she is already there by now. He takes the keys and slips in and out of sleep while the younger men watch the game to its conclusion.

The other women rejoin the men, and they talk about the way Penns Castle used to be, the old times that link them. Wat mentions the new DrugWorld, which most in the group seem to support.

"Hell," Ray says, "they're just trying to make a living like everybody else. It's legal; what else you want?"

"It's a good thing Blanchard isn't here," Willa says. "She'd be ready to fight you right now."

There is laughter from all the adults except Neil and David.

It's almost an hour later, fully dark, when the two of them leave.

Everyone overloads them with hugs and handshakes and turned-down offers of enough food to last them until Christmas. Still, Neil has the feeling that the conversation will be easier, that the whole room will sigh in unison, when he is gone. He wonders if he is getting paranoid.

The sad truth he knows but won't share, though, is that he really doesn't know these people any more. They are family, and they bear him no particular ill will, that he can tell. He wishes sometimes he had been like Tom, always in Penns Castle, always of it. He wishes he were capable of bringing back a time when he bent down to take small hands and guide them across streets, when he tied toddlers' shoes, when he bathed small faces and feet and backsides, when small milk-breathed Willa and Millie and Tom kissed him goodnight.

But he, and they, have long since lost all that. Short of staying in Penns Castle, Neil doesn't really know how the hell he could have kept it from happening.

When they pull into the driveway, the only lights still on are the one in the front of Penn's Castle and the one upstairs, in Blanchard's bedroom.

Neil knocks on her door and asks if she's all right. She says she is, that's she's just exhausted "from all those damn Beauchamps."

"Just let me rest a few minutes," she says. "You all fix yourselves a drink or something."

Neil turns to walk down the dark hallway to the stairs.

"Neil," she calls after him.

"Yes."

"Would you get some of that dog food in the pantry next to the sink, and feed Cully?"

NINETEEN

AT FIRST, IN his dream, he is back in Mundy, and the relentless blaring is the prison alarm system, the guards screwing with them as usual for no good reason, robbing them of precious unconsciousness.

Then, it is an alarm clock. He flails about, futilely searching by touch for the button that will make the world silent again.

By the time he is almost awake, he knows it is something else. The ancient walls of his room pulse red in rhythm with the noise.

He manages to work himself out of bed, fearing that some still-lit cigarette of Blanchard's has ignited the old house. When he looks out the window facing Castle Road, he sees that it is indeed a fire truck that is creating the hellish sound-and-light show, but before he can turn and run for his door and safety, he realizes that the truck is turning around in the circular drive, leaving rather than arriving. Then he sees that there is a brighter glow than that made by the truck, off to his right, beyond the far reaches of Penn's Castle.

Loud but indistinguishable voices correspond over radios outside. As Neil turns to put on pants and shirt, there's a knock at his door.

"Dad."

"I'm here."

"There's a fire, but it's OK. One of the firemen said it's that drug-whatever building down the road."

Neil opens the door. As David stands there, he puts on his clothes, and the two of them go toward the main entrance, turning on lights as they make their way.

Neil stops at the front door.

"What about Blanchard?"

David shakes his head.

"She wasn't in her room. I knocked, and then I opened the door. She wasn't there."

Neil says nothing. He turns and goes back inside, returning with a flashlight. He motions for David to follow him into the house and out the back door into the garden and the woods beyond.

The evening had been quiet. Blanchard came down to join them around nine, then turned in again shortly before 11. She drank water, claiming that she had overindulged, and she talked mostly about the people with whom they had spent Thanksgiving, with David asking her occasional questions about this or that aspect of Penns Castle and its residents.

After she went to bed again, Neil said he supposed David would be glad to get back to Carly and Frannie and Abbie, whose names he made sure to actually say this time.

"Yeah, I miss all my girls," he said.

"Tell me what they're like."

David looked over at him.

"That's right," he said. "I'd forgotten. You haven't seen Abbie."

"Just pictures. And I haven't seen Frannie since she was six days old."

"Six days old." David shook his head. "Damn."

"There weren't many times I wanted 'em to see me in the last six years."

"Well, they're going to see you, soon. We're going to have you up. I promise you that."

Neil said he thought it might be better if they kept it like it was.

"I'll bet you're a good father," he said to David. "I bet

you're a good husband. You've done better than I ever could. I think your mother must have raised you right.

"I don't want to spoil it, don't want 'em to see what a mess their grandfather is. I want 'em to think all the Beauchamps, since 'way back, were great husbands and fathers."

David looked over at him.

"Do you know, do you have any idea, how much I would have given to be you? To be able to do what you did?"

"That's why you should be careful what you ask for. Any fool can be born able to hit a ball. It's a parlor trick, like being double-jointed or seven feet tall. What you did, that's the trick."

David said it was a trick at which he seemed to be losing his touch.

The last time Neil Beauchamp had been in the same room with his son, before David showed up at Mundy to take him away, Carly had just come home from the hospital with Frannie.

Neil had bought the largest stuffed rabbit he could find; it was larger than Carly herself. He had also stopped for a drink, which became a few drinks, at a bar in Alexandria, and he was slightly unsteady on his feet.

He saw the child, remarking that she looked just like David the first time he saw him.

The chill had already hardened into ice by then. Father and son had only seen each other once since the wedding three years before. It had been, by David's estimate, five years since he had seen his father fully sober.

Carly, who had heard all David's stories, had not even wanted to let his father in the house. She had taken David over into her family and didn't see why he had to even let "the old bastard" in the door.

But Neil was there. He had come in peace, although some-what fortified. After a very few minutes of very small talk, he tried to pick up the rabbit and set it in Frannie's crib, which was smaller than the rabbit itself. Then he tried to set it next to the crib, but in wrestling the monstrosity into the corner, he tripped over the edge of a rocker and fell, he and the rabbit tumbling into and splintering the crib. Neil had ended up under his gift, pieces of wood beside and underneath him.

Carly had come running in, Frannie in her arms. When she saw the Virginia Rail sprawled across her carpet, amid the wreckage of the same crib in which she and her mother before her had once lain, she held the baby in one hand and, with the other, pointed toward the door. It struck Neil as funny, something out of a soap opera or a sit-com, but she just stood there, saying nothing, just pointing. Finally, when he saw that his son was going to say nothing, that indeed he was too embarrassed to say anything or even look at him, Neil got to his knees, then up on his feet, and he left.

Half asleep and night-blind, they are no match for the limbs and briers that lash them as they stumble through the quarter-moon darkness that the flashlight only pricks. The fire in front of them only makes the immediate foreground harder to see.

Neil, who has slightly better night vision, leads. He can hear David curse the branches and thorns. He isn't sure he hasn't led them on a fool's errand, but he feels alive. He's doing something physical, something that will test his body instead of his spirit. He breathes deeply, more deeply, he is sure, than he ever did in Mundy. He feels, he realizes, finally free. The humid night air and the damp leaves smell like lost time.

"You don't think she's out here, do you? Not really?" David asks. He is already out of breath.

"Don't know. She might be."

In another minute, they are within 100 feet of the opening. In the middle of the scoured clay before them, flames are coming out windows and through the burned and collapsing roof of what was soon to be Virginia's 22nd DrugWorld megastore. It reminds Neil of the kind of football-season bonfires they used to have on fall Thursday nights, just across the state highway from where they stand now.

Between the fire, the trucks and the ceaseless radio communication, Neil and David can barely hear each other. They kneel and stare at the fire, which the ever-growing number of county volunteer units is only now beginning to neutralize.

"I hope to hell she's not down there," David says into Neil's ear.

Neil just shakes his head and looks around, shining the flashlight cautiously at waist level. He is awake enough to know he does not want to be found anywhere nearly this incriminating for a very long time.

It takes him three circular passes to spot her.

He thinks he sees something more pale than the trees, 50 feet to their right. When he brings the light back, there she is.

Blanchard is sitting on a stump, her elbows on her knees, her chin resting on her folded hands. She might be watching a play or a ball game. She looks as much at peace as Neil ever remembers seeing her.

She doesn't even seem to know they're there, but when they get about 10 feet away, she turns toward them, not spooked at all. She smiles and yawns.

They kneel beside her for several silent minutes as the fire is gradually reduced, its devastation complete.

"Well," Blanchard says finally, "I suppose we ought to be getting back. It was a hell of a show, though, wasn't it?"

They help her to her feet, but she leads them back, without benefit of a flashlight, going so fast that she has to stop twice and wait for them.

When they reach the back door, she stops and bends down to untie and then take off the pair of men's shoes.

"We might want to throw these away," she says, and leaves Neil holding the oversized brogans. "You all might want to clean the mud off yours, too."

When the two men get inside, Blanchard is in the process of locking the front door.

"I swear," she tells them, stopping on the third step up the stairs, "I believe I could sleep a week."

Neil is suddenly shaking, colder than he had been outside. He is afraid he might be coming down with the flu.

He and David turn out the lights and, without saying a word, go back to bed as if they had only gotten up for a midnight snack or a quick trip to the bathroom.

Under the covers, Neil shivers and waits for the doorbell to ring. At some merciful point, he falls asleep.

TWENTY

RUNNING WATER WAKES him up.

He rolls over and looks at the clock beside his bed. He has not slept five hours, and even that rest was disturbed by dreams of fire and prison.

He is exhausted, but he has to get up.

For one thing, he can smell the smoke, feels as if it is so ingrained in his skin that any deputy sheriff looking for an arsonist would have to look no farther.

He must wash himself clean. Maybe he can burn his clothes. Whoever is in the bathroom must have the same idea.

Five minutes later, David knocks softly.

"Dad?"

"Yes."

"Shower's all yours."

Neil is out of bed so quickly that the blood rushes to his head and he has to sit down. Then he realizes that it is not him, or at least not just him: The entire house smells of ashes. It has seeped through closed windows and under doors somehow.

He makes his way to the bathroom.

The face in the mirror startles him. He's getting used to looking old, but he's also dirty. He must have stumbled somewhere in their scramble through the woods and scraped himself. He has scratches on his forehead and the side of his neck. There is dried blood on his shirt collar. And he needs a shave.

He takes a quick shower, scrubbing himself raw, almost exhausting such warmth as Penn's Castle's water heater can produce.

When he's dressed, he goes down to the front door and walks outside.

A front must have passed through during the early morning hours. It's raining, the kind of soft, steady rain that will pace itself and last the day.

The air is thick with smoke, held down by the damp. To his right, he can see a haze hanging over the woods, settled into the tops of the trees. He can hear, again, the harsh squawk of men talking over radios.

Back inside, he finds David sitting in the dining room, alone at the big table. He's made coffee, and Neil gets himself a cup.

"Want to walk down and see what's left?" David asks him.

"No."

"Hell, Dad, they're not going to think you did it. For all we know, she didn't even do it. Maybe it just caught fire."

They hadn't asked Blanchard the night before, hadn't really wanted to know how she came to be sitting on that stump.

"Yeah," Neil says, "maybe it was just an accident."

But when he was helping Blanchard up from that stump, he could smell the gasoline. He imagines David could, too.

"You might want to clean your shoes off," Neil says. "I hope she's thrown hers away."

"We went to watch the fire, Dad. We've got a valid reason to have clay on our shoes."

They sit quietly for a few moments. David gets them both another cup of coffee.

"I've got to go. The car's ready. They're even going to bring it over here, believe it or not. I guess one mechanic's going to follow the other one and drive him back. Six hundred and twenty-five dollars. Thank God for VISA."

Neil says he's sorry he got him into so much trouble.

"Well," David says, "at least we got to do something together." They both smile.

After a few more moments of silence, David says, "Dad?" in a tone that makes Neil brace himself.

Still, at this late date, he has to try.

"Yes, son?"

"I need to know some things."

Neil waits, barely even breathing.

"I found a scrapbook, in the library. There were things in there that Blanchard wrote about you. . . when you were young." He has lowered his voice.

Neil tells him he and Blanchard were always close, that he supposed she looked up to him, for some reason. But he doesn't really know what David has read.

"Were you and she ever, you know, intimate?"

Neil denies this, again too quickly. Then he looks away. He can feel his face burning.

"There are things, David . . . If you live long enough, you do things you'd do differently if you had another chance. But you usually don't get another chance."

David puts his hand on his father's forearm.

"It's OK, Dad. I just want to know who you are. It's not like you were real brother and sister or anything. . ."

Neil jerks his arm away and looks out the window. His hands are shaking, and he puts the cup down.

"Don't you ever tell another living soul," he says, looking at David with red, moist eyes.

David promises, then speaks again, not sure he can press it any farther.

"Well, then, I guess that explains about the house, then."

Neil looks at him.

"The house?"

"Penn's Castle. This." David waves his arms around. "I suppose it is better for appearances to do it the way you did."

Neil asks him what the hell he's talking about.

"Dad, Jack Stoner knows the lawyer that drew up the will. I just hope he doesn't blab it to everybody in Richmond."

Neil just stares, first at David and then out the window, as his son tells him that James Penn never meant to give his only living son a red cent.

"She didn't," Neil says at last. "Why would she do that? She didn't owe me a thing."

"That's a lie and you know it."

They both jump. David spills some of his coffee. They never heard her coming.

"David," Blanchard says, standing over them like some apparition, wearing the same clothes, still smelling of smoke and gasoline, that she was wearing when they found her, "you need to know something about your father. You need to know what kind of man he is."

"Don't, Blanchard," Neil begs her, but it's no use.

"Let me tell you why your daddy deserves at least half this damn mausoleum, no matter what James Blackford Penn did or didn't do."

And so she tells the story, the one she has wanted to drop on some other living soul, the dead weight she has carried for two long years. Neil walks away from the table for most of it, wandering the near reaches of the house. Rain drips off the slate roof and splashes on to the stone outside.

That night, he had not planned to leave his apartment. But he was open to suggestions.

Neil Beauchamp was 60 years old, seriously committed to Letting Go, no Rail any more in deed or appearance. He was not a man who relished a good book or watched much television. Naturally shy, he most easily entertained himself in places where people laughed, alcohol was served and tongues were loosened. He had proved himself singularly incapable of being fit company for his wife or son, but others, on an occasional basis, found him interesting, amusing. Night by night, he devalued his legend through drunken familiarity.

On many nights, like this one, he would say to himself that he was not going out, when what he really meant was, he was not going out unless someone called.

This night, Blanchard called.

He had not heard from her in at least a month. Both her parents were dying, or "failing," as their cousins put it. Blanchard, who too often was not totally able to take care of herself, had to deal with doctors and live-in care-givers and the smell of oncoming death.

Neil had meant to call her, but he hadn't.

She wanted someone to have dinner with, she said. She was sick and tired of spending so much time around sick people. Many of Blanchard's old friends had become ex-friends, either because they avoided her or because they had crossed her in real or imagined ways.

She told Neil, as she had often told him before, that he was the only one she could really count on. It made him uneasy when she said that. He knew just how undependable he had been.

"Come on," she said. "Let's go to Chiocca's."

It was one of Neil's favorites, only three blocks from his apartment. It had the best sandwiches and the coldest beer in town, and everyone knew Neil Beauchamp, still called him "Rail," as almost no one else did any more.

Two televisions — not the jumbo sets they put in the self-styled "sports bars," but the kind Neil had in his living room — were usually showing some game or another, and the people there could comment knowledgeably on whatever was transpiring. Neil wished his late sports bar had had half as much atmosphere as Chiocca's.

He said he'd meet her there. He walked over and had already enjoyed one Miller High Life sitting at the bar when he saw her walking down the stone steps from the street.

She had gone there with him once before and found the low ceiling slightly claustrophobic. She didn't know the people, but it was Neil's bar, and she wanted his company.

She soon caught up with him, four beers each, with a pastrami on rye (hers) and a carnivore's delight known as the Beast (his) somehow consumed amid the talk (mostly hers).

"Let's go somewhere else," she said, stubbing out her sixth cigarette.

"Sure," Neil said. He thought that, if Blanchard was going to smoke a cigarette every 15 minutes, maybe they could go somewhere that had higher ceilings.

They made their way through the Fan, to Buddy's, then John and Norman's, finally to a place on Main Street where they could sit on the patio and enjoy the cool relief between two hot Richmond days, even feel the ghost of a breeze.

Neil was drinking one beer to Blanchard's two by now, not having even one at Buddy's but settling for a Coke instead, because he knew that he would have to — as he had done before — drive her several miles home, then call a taxi to take him back to his apartment.

"What the hell," she said to him when he wondered if she didn't want to slow down a little. "I'm a little too old to be developing good habits, don't you think?"

Neil didn't answer, but he was beyond trying very hard to discourage her.

They didn't leave the last bar until nearly one a.m. Blanchard had parked four blocks back, and by the time they got there, she swore she was sober enough to drive.

"No," Neil said. "Give me the keys."

"Come and get 'em," Blanchard said. She grinned at him as she reached inside the waist of her skirt and, after some fumbling and wiggling, brought the hand back out, empty. "Look, Ma. No keys."

She would occasionally do something like that, although as they got older, Neil thought that surely it must be more for show than lust. Still, it unsettled him. He liked Blanchard, loved her he supposed, but he did not want this.

"Blanchard," he said, and the look he gave her must have had enough pity and disgust in it to set her off.

"You think I'm some drunken old slut," she said, raising her voice as he tried to calm her. "Get in the goddamn car. I'm taking you home. You're no fun." Neil could hear other, younger voices laughing somewhere close behind him.

He should have taken the keys from her, even if he had to pull her panties down to retrieve them. But he was exhausted, exasperated, and nearly as drunk as she was.

So he got in on the passenger's side, as Blanchard was starting the car. He could have walked home from there, but he thought he ought to at least ride with her, in case there was trouble.

The Penns lived outside the city limits, on a curving road that drew the richest of the old-family city emigrants and the out-of-towners buying bargains: Southern real estate with Northeastern money.

The people who lived there had resisted widening or straightening the road, fearing that the teenagers and college students would only go faster if they were able to. It claimed a few of the careless and unlucky every year, but not enough to effect what people along the road wanted least in all aspects of life — change.

By the time Blanchard approached the last curve before the driveway to her home, it was 1:25, the report said later. She and Neil were arguing, or rather she was arguing, incensed that he had suggested she should slow down. The report estimated the Lexus was going 60 miles an hour, 15 miles over the limit even for the straightaways.

Ten minutes before, state trooper Lacy Haithcock had pulled a car full of teenagers, sure that they must have been drinking, or at least that they would be less likely to drink in the near future if he scared the hell out of them.

He did not smell alcohol, and the four girls were almost in tears. They had been going no more than five miles an hour over the limit, and trooper Haithcock let them go with a stern warning.

Returning to his car, he had to walk on the pavement, just over the white line. He didn't even think about it. His blue light was on. Anyone could see it from four hundred yards.

Except that the curve cut that down to a hundred yards. Except that Blanchard was looking at Neil, screaming at him, and he was distracted by her.

The car clipped Lacy Haithcock, knocking his body a full 50 feet across the road and into the ditch on the other side.

Blanchard had also sideswiped the patrol car, damaging Neil's side of the Lexus so badly that, when they skidded to a stop a few hundred yards beyond, he could not open his door.

"Oh, shit," Blanchard said, pure panic in her eyes. "Oh, shit! Goddamn!" The car had choked out, and while Neil was trying to open the wrecked door, she started it again and went the short distance to the Penns' driveway.

Neil told her to stop, tried to grab the steering wheel, but she pushed him off and managed to avoid the trees on both sides of the drive. No more than a minute after Lacy Haithcock was struck and killed, she was sitting in her wrecked car, safe outside her own home.

She opened the garage door from the car, but then Neil finally got control of her hand, turned off the ignition and wrested the keys from her.

"Blanchard," he said, grabbing the other hand, too, "we can't do this. We can't."

She said nothing, but she finally got out of the car, and he followed her.

The flood lights revealed the extent of the damage: a broken headlight, dents and scrapes running down the whole right side of the car, and a large, round dent across the front.

Neil looked up from where he kneeled, by the part of Blanchard Penn's Lexus with which Lacy Haithcock's body had collided.

She was standing in the middle of the paved parking lot, looking off into dark, searching for something. And then she started whistling, and calling her dog's name.

Neil knew, then, what came next.

He might have acted differently at a different stage of his life. If there had been a wife or children to protect. If he had still been the Virginia Rail, feared by American League pitchers, beloved by a city. If he had not, long before, slipped into the Time of Letting Go, when he had come to feel that some kind of punishment for Neil Beauchamp was long overdue.

Had he driven Blanchard back to the scene, from which he could already hear a siren approaching, he had no doubt that she would have taken the blame. If nothing else, she was too drunk to do otherwise.

"Stay here," he told her. He still had the key in his hand. She half-turned toward him and nodded, then looked back to the darkness.

Neil Beauchamp stepped into Blanchard's guilty, damaged gray Lexus, and he drove it back to the accident scene. He did not refuse to take the breathalyzer test, which showed him to be well past the limit for legal drunkenness as determined by the Commonwealth of Virginia. He did not offer, from then through the sentencing, anything except regret and sorrow.

He saw her once while he was awaiting trial. Neither of them acknowledged what happened on that June night. Blanchard has only hinted at it, alluded to it, until now. She would tell Neil, over and over, during prison visits, how sorry she was, never really saying for what exactly, as he shushed her and told her it was OK.

When Blanchard is through, she sits, hard and suddenly, in the largest chair in her living room. She is crying, great streaks of water running down her face, which is unadorned and suddenly old in the dreary morning light.

TWENTY-ONE

THEY ARE SHELTERED just inside the large, open front doors of Penn's Castle, looking out at the soft, steady rain. It will make it easier, David thinks. No lingering goodbyes, just a mad dash across the gravel and away from the Virginia Rail.

"So," he says to his father, "it's settled, then. I'll talk to Carly, and you'll have two weeks to square things with Blanchard. OK?"

Neil turns.

"You're sure you want to do this?" he asks, again. "I don't even know if they'll let me, the parole office and all . . ."

David walks the long step toward him and takes him by the shoulders, a strangely physical move for his son, Neil thinks.

"Again: Let me worry about that, Dad. We'll get it done."

Neil nods again.

"Two weeks," David says again, and then he runs into the rain. In seconds, he's headed north.

They've had time enough to talk already.

After Blanchard left the room "to make myself presentable," they were alone for an hour.

At first, Neil only wanted to deny that any of it had happened the way Blanchard said.

"If you've got any sympathy," he told David at last, "save it for that state trooper. Isn't anything going to bring him back. I've got some time left, at least."

He had never tithed, never gone to church after adults stopped making him go, not even when Kate was taking

David. Now, though, his goal was to give 10 percent of anything he could make, signing autographs, bagging groceries, whatever he could do to earn money, to Lacy Haithcock's family. He still had a life insurance policy that he had somehow managed to keep during all the letting-go years. Blanchard had made the payments for him while he was at Mundy. Before he went in, he had changed the beneficiary to Warren Haithcock.

"It isn't anything," he said when he told David what he planned to do. "It isn't anything next to losing a son."

David looked at him, but Neil spoke first.

"I know. I'm a fine one to talk about losing sons, when I gave you up so easy. Kate and I should've had you when I was 40. We could've done things together. . ." He had to stop there.

"Hell," David told him, "we still can."

And he made up the plan for the rest of their lives, right there in Blanchard Penn's living room. He did it without asking for Neil's input, without consulting Carly, without considering his own unsettled future.

He and Carly consulted on everything. He never made a major decision without getting her approval. But a golfing buddy of his had told him once that no marriage is secure unless both people can declare a state of emergency and assume dictatorial powers when the need demands it.

"But it can't be one or the other, it's got to be both," he had said. "You can't do it but maybe once every five years. And if you play that trump card, you can be sure she's going to have one that she'll play down the road, and you better be ready to grin and bear it when she does."

David hoped, as he explained his plan to Neil, that Carly would understand the depth of his need to do what he was planning to do.

There were one-bedroom apartments near them, not far from the river, that Neil Beauchamp's baseball pension might pay for. There were surely more opportunities for a legend in the Washington suburbs than in Penns Castle.

He knew what Carly would say, at first, about how poorly Neil Beauchamp had cared for his only son when he had truly needed care, how he was coming around now with nothing to offer but old age.

And David was prepared to tell her that he didn't care. Screw the past. We'll start with now and see where it goes.

When Blanchard came back down, looking almost as good as she had when they had arrived on her doorstep on Monday, David told her his plan.

Neil was silent, not offering so much as an encouraging glance or nod. He was in no way sure that what David envisioned could happen. He still remembered the look on Carly's face the last time they had seen each other. And he was certain he did not deserve such kindness as his son was offering. He also wondered what would become of Blanchard, still smelling of smoke. He knew, though, that he would not refuse his son's offer, did not in any way want to.

Blanchard argued that there was no way the parole board would let him leave the Richmond area. David pointed out that Alexandria was, after all, in the same state.

"This is his home," she said. "He'll fare a hell of a lot better here than in some big, scary city." David argued that Neil had spent most of his adult life in "big, scary cities," and that Alexandria wasn't Washington.

She saved her best ammunition for last.

"Who was there for him, when he went to prison?" she asked. "Who visited him?"

David was silent.

"I want to take care of him, David." She was pleading now. "I owe him that. I've sworn I'd spend the rest of my life taking care of him, like he's taken care of me."

"Wait."

David and Blanchard had both forgotten Neil was still in the room, until he spoke.

"Blanchard," he said, turning to her, "let's see how it goes. If David wants me to come with him for a while, I think I'm going to give it a try. For a while."

David started to speak, but Neil held up his hand.

"We'll spend a couple of weeks here together, and then I'll go up there for a little bit, just to see how it goes. They probably won't let me do it anyhow, and David's family'll probably ship me back here in a box in under a week when they see what a horse's ass I am."

"Don't try to jolly me," Blanchard said. She turned away.

"Why don't you go ahead and pack?" Neil told David.

Once they were alone, Neil took Blanchard's hands in his.

"I don't know what's going on," he told her. "I feel like I've landed on another planet. Last Sunday, I was wearing blue denim with a number on it. But he's my son, Blanchard. He's my son."

"And what am I?"

"You're my best friend. I'm going to spend the next two weeks with you, and then we'll just see what happens. Like I said, they'll probably be damn glad to have me back down here inside of a week."

They sat in silence for a long time. She moved next to him on the couch, sliding under his arm, leaning against him so close he could feel her heartbeat.

"Always come back here, Neil," she said.

He nodded.

Tom drops by and seems genuinely sorry to have missed David.

"I hope he'll come to see us more now," he says.

"He's coming back in two weeks to take Neil away," Blanchard tells him.

"Up north?"

"Just Alexandria," Neil says, "and probably not for good."

Blanchard is biting her lip.

Tom sits with them for a few minutes, talking about the fire, but the weather seems to have put a damper on conversation.

When he gets up to leave, Neil walks with him as far as the front door.

He looks at Tom, short and wide and happy, never outstanding in any endeavor except endurance.

"Maybe you'd like to go deer hunting with us next week," Tom tells him, and Neil, who has never cared for hunting, says that would be fine, as long as they don't expect him to shoot anything.

Tom is standing, watching the rain drip from the overhang.

"You know," he says, jamming his hands in his pockets, "I don't think I've ever really thanked you for all you did for us, you know, back then."

"I didn't do anything for you. I left home and sent a little money. You're the one that stayed and made everything work."

"Well," Tom says, as he prepares to dash for his truck, "if I'd have been you, been able to do what you did, I'd have done the same thing. Might not even have sent any money home. Might've changed my name."

He laughs and, pulling his jacket up over his head, leaves Neil standing in the doorway.

Back inside, he sits for a while with Blanchard, who has convinced herself Neil will soon be gone from her forever.

"Blanchard," he says, "there have been years when I didn't see you once. Whole years. This won't be as bad as that, will it?"

"Yes, it will," she says, and then she begins to cry. "This time, I thought I had you back. I thought we would be together."

Neil wonders if Blanchard Penn even sees him, the 1997 Neil Beauchamp, when she looks his way. He wonders if what she sees isn't some apparition from the past. It occurs to him that he might be, to her, inhabiting the same world as Cully.

He is very tired. The one thing he did get enough of in prison was sleep; he's used to nine hours a day, and he is far behind that since coming back to Penn's Castle.

He stands up, aching like the old man he supposes he is now.

"I'm beat," he tells her. "If you don't mind, I'm going to take a little nap. If I'm not up by four, wake me up.

"We'll have a good, long talk then."

She nods her head.

"Please, Blanchard," he says. "Give me a smile. I'm not going for good. I promise."

It seems to be an effort, but she does smile, and tells him to sleep tight.

TWENTY-TWO

INSIDE THE MCDONALD'S, 30 miles away from Penn's Castle, David finds himself in the line from hell.

He had expected the lunch crowd to be long gone, but he forgot that it was the day after Thanksgiving.

There must be a mall nearby, because tired women and crying children surround him. The restaurant has made no allowances for this special shopping day, apparently, because only two lines are open, and they move at a maddeningly slow pace. David looks around to see if he is the only one going insane, but the rest just seem to be numb. Even the children's crying has a sameness, a lack of real effort, as if they are crying in their sleep.

When he finally arrives at the front, he gets into an argument with a young man, slack-jawed and unapologetically ignorant, who seems unable to get his order right, despite David's repeating it twice, or make change, despite the computerized cash register.

David snatches the tray of Coke, Quarter Pounder and french fries, spilling some of the soft drink on his sleeve. He can hear the young man laugh behind him, and he wants very much to return and slap him, actually stops for a second intending to do that before he gets a grip on his temper and finds a ketchup-stained table.

He is out of sorts, and he can't really lay it all off to hunger and lack of sleep, or on long lines.

He called Carly before he left and talked to her and the girls. He has not told his wife yet that the famous Virginia Rail soon will be living in their very own neighborhood. That can wait. Talking to the three of them made him all the more eager to get back, and he supposes that part of his impatience is the anticipation of seeing them again soon.

"Easy," he says to himself. "Easy. Home before you know it."

But there's something else. He feels as if he has just awakened from a powerful dream, the kind that leaves him nearly in tears while the particulars of it fade by the second.

He is back on the road five minutes after he sits down to eat, having spent four times as long waiting for his food as he did eating it.

He is still bothered, and it takes a conscious effort to keep from converting his discomfort into road rage. He repeats his new mantra: "Home before you know it. Home before you know it." He finds the Richmond public radio station, and the music soothes him.

He hasn't been back on the interstate for more than 10 minutes when the dog appears in front of him, on the shoulder of the road.

He's gotten into one of the blessed interludes that appear out of nowhere on I-95, a stretch where there's not one car or truck for half a mile in front of him, no need to tailgate or switch lanes for at least a couple of minutes.

And then the dog is there, snuffling its way across the highway, maybe tracking deer or rabbit. He checks his rearview mirror and slows to 60, easing into the slowest lane, but the dog goes forward, now one hundred yards ahead, ambling out of David's lane and into the middle one.

Out of nowhere, the low, black car with D.C. tags appears in his rearview mirror, going at least 100, David estimates, when it hits the dog just as it reaches the fast lane. The car never even slows, and the dog is pitched into the air, dead before it hits the pavement. And in that split second, David sees that it is a beagle.

Now he remembers.

It happened before he left Blanchard's, in the very few minutes when he was alone with her. He was uneasy, like a man who is about to steal his host's silverware.

While he was sitting there, she got up and went to the kitchen. He heard her banging around as if she were looking for something, and then she came out and headed for the back door.

He asked if he could help, and she waved him off.

"No. I'll be back in a second. I've just got to take care of Cully."

He heard her call the dog, and then lower her voice, as if Cully had actually come to her.

"That's OK, boy," he heard her say. "It'll be OK now. Good boy. It won't be much longer. Good boy."

It hadn't seemed worth noting.

And, until now, he had not thought about the thing that has been nibbling into his brain since he left Penn's Castle, the thing that finally reveals itself to him now, makes him swerve in front of another driver into the slow lane and then onto the exit, going 70 and braking hard, angry horn blasts trailing him.

He had gone into the kitchen, just before he left, to get a glass of water. And there it was, only mildly strange to him then.

There was dry dog food spilled on the floor. He hadn't known that Blanchard carried it that far. And on the kitchen counter, directly above the dog food, was the still-open container of rat poison.

In his dream, Neil is back in William Beauchamp's house.

The house was heated by gas, which they also used for cooking. One of Neil's chores was to light the stove before breakfast and before dinner. He hated that stove, with its pilot light that had to be re-ignited every time they cooked a meal, the "whump" that always jarred his nerves when he reached in with the match. The smell of the gas before he lit it had a sickening odor, one he has always associated with danger.

Once, when he was 12, he saw the remains of a house blown up by leaking gas. There was nothing left except sticks.

He would never let Kate have gas put into any of their homes.

Now, he wakes up to that smell from long ago, only stronger. He finally realizes that he is not in his stepfather's house.

He wonders if he is dreaming, but the stench seems too real. In the distance he can hear a woman's voice singing something he can't quite make out.

He raises himself out of his bed and listens. The hairs on his arms are standing up. He knows he is at least 60 feet from the front door, and that the window behind him is closed.

He sees only one option. He drops as silently as he can to the floor, and he runs. He has not run in more than two years, and he is 62 years old. But he has heard enough; and the singing seems to be getting nearer. It is a pleasant voice, the voice of a once-beautiful woman who has reached and passed some crisis, whose mind is made up.

He charges out the half-open door and then down the hall as if he is trying to score from second on a left-field single, expecting every step to be his last, assuming he will be blown apart.

David is stuck in traffic, stopped dead a mile east of the Castle Road intersection. When the second fire truck goes by, forcing cars in the left lane into the median strip, he leaves the Camry and begins running toward the smoke up ahead.

He has returned to Penn's Castle far faster than he left, going 80 on the interstate, 65 in the 45 zone along the state highway.

And yet, as he gets nearer, running past surprised motorists, some outside their cars gawking at the spectacle and then at him, he sees he didn't drive fast enough.

"Go, O.J.!" one wit calls behind him, evoking a television commercial from the distant past and getting some laughs. Others honk their horns.

He is out of shape, and he can hear his own breath, coming in a ragged two-two count, then a one-one as he tries to suck in enough air to continue up the hill.

He crosses the highway at the intersection, running past a deputy sheriff who whistles angrily but helplessly. He passes the ruins of DrugWorld, still smoldering in the light rain.

Soon, he is running past fire trucks and rescue vehicles, and as he gets nearer, hoses snake across the road toward the place where Penn's Castle had stood a few minutes before. The abrasive blasts of sirens pierce the air.

In the road, and along the sides, David dodges pieces of stone that were hewn from an English quarry almost five centuries before, that survived disassembly and a trip across an ocean to be rejoined on a Virginia hillside and, finally, blown apart.

David stops as he gets to the driveway. He can run no farther.

He collapses into the gravel, defeated.

233

TWENTY-THREE

Saturday, 11 a.m.

It isn't much of a parade.

Half a dozen floats, pulled by tractors, are interspersed with nine marching bands from every high school willing to send one, plus the convertibles with local politicians and their wives and children throwing candy canes and tangerines to a crowd that never surpasses one thousand.

There was considerable sentiment for canceling or postponing it, but everything had already been arranged, and it would have been hard to get in touch with the bands on such short notice.

The parade starts at the bottom of the hill on Dropshaft Road, by Pride Creek.

Normally, it would run through the middle of town, past Penn Station and Tom Beauchamp's hardware store, then make a right turn and continue up Castle Road, past Penn's Castle, crossing Route 56 and disembarking, as the band director put it, at the high school.

This year, they have made one concession to the events of the past 24 hours. Instead of turning right, the parade will turn left and go past the strip mall, close to the new homes along the golf course. Then, it will loop around Lake Pride before disbanding. Many of the newer residents had been lobbying for such a route, arguing that the tax dollars that pay the town's officials' small stipend come mostly from the big homes near the golf course.

The parade starts uneventfully, but there is a restlessness, an irritability to it, as if spectators and participants alike, bent on having a Christmas parade, would as soon have it over.

The sun is out, but it has turned cold, and many of the parents and children alongside Dropshaft Road are wearing their winter coats for the first time.

Before the parade has fully passed through the little downtown, a deputy has forced one band to pull off to the side of the street after warning its director once already to "step it up" and keep pace with the Miss Junior Penns Castle float that it follows. The director argues with the deputy and is arrested. People in the crowd boo.

And then, with the parade almost past the old railroad station, much of it already headed south toward the lake, the deer appears.

It must have been roused out of the thick woods behind the Presbyterian church by all the noise, people would say later.

The first anyone sees of it, it is hurtling in a blind panic across the street, between the Elks Club float and the last convertible, which is carrying Old Saint Nick himself.

The Beauchamp family is represented by Patti and Rae Dawn, who insisted on seeing the parade.

"Look!" the little girl cries out as the deer stops on the pavement, his hooves skidding, hemmed in by buildings. The man pulling the Elks Club float stops, and Santa Claus' driver almost rams it from behind.

The deer paces back and forth once, quickly, then runs back across the street, this time behind Santa Claus. It streaks mindlessly straight for Penn Station and crashes through the diner's plate-glass window. Patrons come running and falling out the door.

It is finally the cook who somehow maneuvers the animal from the back of the building, where it has destroyed several tables and a juke box, and gets it to leap back out the now-windowless window opening. The crowd outside spooks the animal, which turns and runs, seemingly no worse off than it was five minutes before, back into the hardwoods.

The little girl tugs on the sleeve of the stranger standing next to her and her mother.

"That was Dasher," she says, wide-eyed, and the man nods and pats her head.

David passes the King's Dominion sign. The traffic is starting to thin out from the merge with 295 and won't be really bad again until he gets near the giant shopping complex that is the state's largest tourist attraction.

He eases his grip on the steering wheel and lets out a long breath.

He looks to his right, where the once-famous Virginia Rail has fallen fast asleep.

The blast came no more than a second after Neil hit the ground, rolling him like a log into the brush beyond the driveway. All the way out of the house and into the yard, he had expected it, expected death. But when it had not yet come by the time he cleared the gravel drive, he dove to the wet clay, in time.

He lay there, fetal, for several seconds, deaf and afraid to look. He could feel the thump of large objects nearby. As soon as he opened his eyes, he saw that the building blocks of Penn's Castle had fallen all around him. Some of the pieces of stone would be found more than 200 yards away. One crashed through the roof of a Castle Road home, destroying a La-Z-Boy recliner that was (miraculously, everyone agreed) unoccupied at the time.

He wandered through the brush along the edge of the yard, too stunned to call attention to himself. He felt as if he were already dead, walking in a silent world obscured by smoke. He could see enough of the space before him to know that Penn's Castle had disappeared.

The first to arrive were people whose car windshields had been shattered by the blast. Two of them had driven into the ditch, blown there by the explosion, they would swear later. The firemen and rescue squad were on the scene within five minutes.

Neil sat down by a tree on the edge of the woods, not far from the road, unnoticed. He had been sitting there for almost half an hour when he saw his son run into the driveway, then stop. David's appearance only added to his belief that he was either dead or dreaming, although the fact that he already had regained some of his hearing made him think he might be alive and awake. Neil felt that, if he was not dreaming, he should warn David to take it easy; he looked as if he were about to have a heart attack.

David collapsed to the ground, and Neil, bleeding and limping, got up and went to his son's aid.

"Are you okay?" he asked, and David looked up, speechless, his mouth open.

"Careful," Neil said, as his son pulled him to the ground, hugging his aching ribs. He said it again, louder, to be sure he was heard. "I'm OK. But Blanchard . . ."

David can't believe he was able to leave Penns Castle with his father. After his experience with car repair, he had become convinced that nothing happened quickly or effortlessly in his father's hometown.

But nobody seemed interested in locking up Neil Beauchamp, or even holding him for questioning beyond an hour or so at the hospital, where stitches were administered to his right arm and forehead. He was advised, before they released him, that he might suffer some permanent hearing loss.

The police said they would be asking more about the explosion later, and David gave them his address in Alexandria.

Neil, with David helping, told his story. Tom, who had come running almost as quickly as the first fire truck, added that Blanchard Penn had been somewhat "beside herself" of late, that they were afraid she might do something like this.

Neil assumed that the detective questioning him did not recognize him in time to make real trouble.

What they found of Blanchard Penn mostly consisted of scraps of cloth here and there, a shoe she was apparently wearing.

That night, at Wat and Millie's house, Neil broke down.

No one had ever seen him like this, not even the late Blanchard on her visits to Mundy. He excused himself from the den where he had been sitting gingerly in an easy chair and went to his guest room after tears had begun running down his cheeks in the middle of a TV sitcom no one was watching. For an hour, he wouldn't let even David in. He cried for Blanchard, whom he could not save, whom he didn't even try to save, he realized.

David is sure that he and Neil will be visited, very soon, by detectives, and he worries that the authorities will use any excuse they can find to make life hard for a man with Neil's record.

He wonders what they might surmise when and if they find a gas can or incriminating footprints leading from the ruined DrugWorld to the leveled Penn's Castle.

Still, he is buoyant. He doesn't know why, but he starts whistling, driving up I-95, a road that normally makes him grind his teeth. He believes, against all odds, that he and his family, including the Virginia Rail, will land on their feet.

Neil wakes up and looks over at his son, an unspoken question on his face. He has been dreaming of prison again. Looking over his shoulder, he half expects that they will be pulled over, that he will be handcuffed and hauled back to Richmond, to jail. He can't hear well at all, and he wonders if he doesn't have a concussion. He had three of them while he was playing baseball, and they felt like this.

"Don't worry," David tells him. "The worst is behind us now." And he resumes whistling. Through the fog, it sounds to Neil like "Blue Skies."

With the cold Virginia morning rolling past his window, Neil Beauchamp leans against the door and is soon asleep again.

Later, when they shift lanes, his weight falls toward his son, who reaches out with his right hand and catches him.